NEXT GIRL MISSING

A THOMAS SHEPHERD CRIME THRILLER
BOOK 8

DAN PADAVONA

GET A FREE BOOK!

I'm a pretty nice guy once you look past the grisly images in my head. Most of all, I love connecting with awesome readers like you.

Join my VIP Reader Group and get a FREE serial killer thriller for your Kindle.

Get My Free Book

www.danpadavona.com/thriller-readers-vip-group/

1

Wolf Lake lay cradled in the Finger Lakes valley. The water mirrored the blue sky and promised an endless summer. The town, a patchwork of quaint houses and well-tended gardens, hummed with the day-to-day life of its residents. Here, people greeted each other by name and conversations spread like dandelion seeds.

"Race you to the big oak!"

Emma Walsh's voice broke through the morning calm as she sprinted ahead, her curly red hair creating a fiery trail behind her.

"Hey, no fair," Hannah called out. She chased after her friend, her own braid whipping in the wind. "You got a head start."

They arrived at the tree and gasped for air. Their shoulders shook with giggles. Leaning against the bark, they shared a knowing look that spoke of years of friendship.

The girls had grown up in the same neighborhood and spent most of their twelve-year-old lives together. They could finish each other's sentences, and both loved ice cream, bicycling, and listening to a new band called Coldplay when their parents weren't around to pass judgment.

Hannah panted. "Okay, you win this time."

"Always do."

The school bell rang in the distance. They were late. With synchronized movements born from countless repetitions, they gathered their backpacks and joined the stream of children rushing toward the schoolhouse.

Inside the classroom, they sat side by side, desks touching. Under the watchful eyes of historical figures framed on the walls, scribbled notes passed back and forth.

"Summer's almost here," Hannah whispered. “Freedom.”

"Can't wait. Swimming every day."

"Hamburgers and french fries."

"Fireworks," Emma said, and they shared a smile.

As it always did this time of year, when the calendar promised lazy afternoons before long, the school day dragged on. Until the dismissal bell released them into the world, where they walked home, shoulder to shoulder. Conversations turned from homework woes to the grand plans that only the cusp of summer could inspire.

"Let's build a fort in the woods," Emma said. “My dad is teaching me to use tools.”

"An impenetrable fortress. No boys allowed." Hannah paused. “Except the cute ones.”

They burst into laughter.

"Secret handshakes?"

"And a flag. Every castle needs a flag."

There was a sense of timelessness in Wolf Lake, a feeling that nothing ever changed, not really.

As they turned down Maple Street, the shadows deepened, stretching across the pavement like fingers. But in the heart of

Wolf Lake, where everyone knew your name and nobody locked their doors, there was nothing to fear.

The girls traveled in comfortable silence until a flicker from a television screen caught their eyes through the Johnsons' living room window.

"Another kid missing in the northern part of the county," Mr. Johnson said from inside. The news anchor's solemn face flashed for a moment before the girls looked away.

"From Brookdale," Hannah said. "That's close to us."

"Kids don't go missing in Wolf Lake. We're safe here."

"I guess," Hannah agreed, but there was a question in her voice that hadn't been there before.

They turned the corner and the subject shifted, as it often did, toward futures painted in broad, hopeful strokes.

"Mom says I need to think about what I want to do when I grow up," Emma said. "I don't understand why. That's like so far into the future that it's ridiculous. Who knows what I'll study in college?"

"I'm going to be a journalist."

"Journalist? Why would you want to be a news reporter?" Emma laughed, shaking her head. "Sounds silly. You should be a doctor or a teacher."

"That's mean. Reporters just report. Journalists tell stories and uncover truths. I want to make a difference."

"Sorry. I didn't realize it meant so much to you."

Hannah's lips pressed into a thin line, but she nodded, letting the moment pass. "Hey, I have to go down Birch Lane today. Mom needs me to pick up milk on the way home."

"Want me to come along?"

"Nah, it's fine. Birch is just a quick detour." Hannah's smile returned, though it didn't quite reach her eyes.

"Are you sure?"

"Positive. See you tomorrow."

With a wave, Hannah turned, leaving Emma to watch her friend's retreating figure.

"Be careful," Emma called after her; the words held an unfamiliar ring of worry.

Hannah's form disappeared around the bend. Ever since they'd overheard the news report coming out of the Johnsons' house, the tranquility that cloaked Wolf Lake felt thinner, like mist dissolving under the scrutiny of the sun. Emma turned toward home.

EMMA AWOKE WITH A START. What time was it?

The red glow bleeding through the window seemed out of place. It wasn't morning. The bedside clock read 7 p.m. How long had she napped?

There were voices coming from the front room. Her parents and someone else. Mrs. Clarke?

The possibility that Mrs. Clarke had brought Hannah with her brought a wave of hope. But the excitement tasted dead on her tongue. Something was wrong.

Emma padded barefoot from the bedroom to the living room. Time became a blur.

"No, she didn't come home with Emma," Mom said to Hannah's mother. When she noticed Emma, she turned to her. "Emma, when was the last time you saw Hannah?"

Why was Mrs. Clarke crying?

"Emma, answer me."

Emma swallowed. "After school. Hannah said she was going to the corner store to pick up milk. What happened? Where is she?"

Each question burst forth with more panic.

The neighborhood sprang into action. Wolf Lake had lost

one of its own, and they would find Hannah and bring her home. Before Sheriff Gray and his deputies arrived, half of Wolf Lake was searching the streets from the village center to the lake shore and forest.

It was dark now. Emma paced the edge of the woods, her sneakers crushing the underbrush. She could feel her heart thumping against her ribs. The night air was cool, but sweat beaded on Emma's forehead, not from exertion but from raw fear.

Why had she been so insistent on taking the usual way home? She should have gone with Hannah.

"Mr. and Mrs. Walsh," Arnie Jenkins said. "Take Emma along the north trail. I'll head towards the Hollow. Shout if you see anything."

Her father grabbed her shoulder and ushered her into a deeper darkness. Things skittered through dead leaves. This wasn't Wolf Lake anymore. It was an evil place out of a Grimm fairytale.

Flashlight beams bobbed in the distance. Sheriff Gray's voice rang out over the others.

The flashlight in her own hand flickered, casting erratic shadows across the ground. She gave it a shake, but the light remained dim. It offered little resistance against the night.

"Where are you, Hannah?" The question escaped her lips. The forest swallowed her voice.

She realized she was crying. Mom stopped and kneeled before her, cupping her face so their eyes met.

“We'll find her, Emma. Don't worry. This time tomorrow, you'll be talking on the phone and laughing about everyone worrying.”

Emma remembered Hannah talking about the future. She wanted to be a journalist, not a reporter. The distinction felt important now, though Emma wasn't sure why.

"Got something," someone on the path said.

A surge of adrenaline propelled Emma forward. She ran towards the voice as branches caught her hair and pulled threads loose from her ponytail.

"It's a backpack," the deputy said.

Emma pushed through the gathering for a closer look. A sickness settled in her stomach.

"That's not Hannah's," Mrs. Clarke said. "Where's my baby? Where is she?"

The woman turned to the others. Blank faces stared back.

Amid the quiet, a knowing terror spread among the onlookers.

Hannah wasn't coming home.

2

"I never saw the patch of mud until I rounded the bend."

LeVar Hopkins' story caused the team to burst into hysterics inside Wolf Lake Consulting. Chelsey was here with Raven, and the two co-owners of the private investigation firm were munching on danishes from The Broken Yolk cafe. Scout, with her hair pulled back in a bun, choked on the treat and leaned over, coughing.

"Let me get this straight," Raven said, unable to keep a straight face. "Thomas sent you on a routine surveillance mission."

"Hundred percent," LeVar said. "Dude was a petty theft suspect, not a hardened criminal."

"Where were you when this happened?"

"I told you. Thomas had me scope out the village park."

Chelsey composed herself and pantomimed seriousness. "Since you wanted to fit in and appear inconspicuous, you went for a jog."

"Isn't that what I said?"

"What happened next?"

LeVar rolled his eyes. He'd told the story twice this morning, yet they acted as if this was a complex mystery. It was March in the Finger Lakes of New York. Over the last month, the snow had melted and caused messy conditions. Just like every spring.

"*Aight*, dawg. Dude took off running. I figured he'd upped his game and snatched a purse. There was shouting."

"Yeah, because a kid scored a goal in a lacrosse game on the other side of the park," Scout said, pointing out the obvious.

He gave her a blank look. "How was I supposed to know there was a game going on? I thought someone needed help."

"So you ran after the perp?"

"Jogged. I was trying to fit in. How many times do you have to repeat myself?"

Raven chewed another piece of danish. "I want to make sure I have this right. You came down the hill, hit the turn, and—"

"Slipped on a slick of mud. Doesn't the village clean those paths? I pay taxes."

"Yeah, we all pay taxes to support sheriff's deputies like you. But I feel like you would make a better circus performer."

He stared at his sister until she laughed. "How was I supposed to know the trail was muddy?"

"It's March, LeVar," Chelsey said. "That's mud season in Upstate New York."

"Tell us the part about how the suspect got away, and you were lying face-down in a mud pit," Scout said.

He lifted his chin. "Yo, I'd rather not."

"But that's the best part of the story."

"Use your imagination." LeVar wiped the corners of his mouth with a napkin. "Pass me another danish."

When would they lose interest in his antics? Everyone screwed up now and then.

"Little brother," Raven said.

He cocked a suspicious eyebrow. "Yeah?"

"Did you at least catch the kid who scored the goal?"

Now they were all laughing. Even LeVar couldn't help himself. Oh, well. It was another morning at the private investigation firm.

"That's one for the books, bro," Raven said while reaching for another treat. "But we should circle back to our security talk."

Chelsey and Raven were upgrading the firm's cameras and alarm system.

“Can't it wait until tomorrow? Y'all are giving me a headache with all this technology talk.”

“Then you won't want to hear about this encryption software I started working with,” Scout said. “This is next-gen stuff, guys. It's going to revolutionize how we handle data encryption.”

“I'm glad you're in charge,” said Chelsey. “The new wave of data encryption is a little above my pay grade.”

“Revolutionize, huh? Give us the rundown. Enlighten us, oh wise one.”

“Imagine a firewall so intuitive that it evolves with each threat. That's just the tip of the iceberg.”

Raven turned toward the girl, skepticism and interest mingling in her eyes. “Security is only as strong as its weakest link. How does it fare against human error?”

"User-friendly interfaces and predictive algorithms catch discrepancies before they become breaches."

"Sounds impressive."

"Pencil in a test run. And Chelsey, about those updates to our current system..."

"Already on it," Chelsey said, pushing back a strand of hair. "I've drafted new protocols. Efficiency is key, but so is adaptability."

"Music to my ears. All right, team. We're running behind on the Mendenhall infidelity investigation, and the new website needs an enhanced sign-up form."

"I've got the website handled," Scout said. "LeVar, can you help me with the back-end code?"

Scout had helped the team upgrade their website and make it interactive, including an AI-based, responsive assistant that answered frequently asked questions.

"I got you," said LeVar.

A whoosh of wind traveled into the main office when the door to Wolf Lake Consulting swung open. Heads turned in unison.

A tall, lean man with sharp features waited at the threshold. His dark hair was combed back with precision, and his eyes scrutinized everything and everyone. A crisp, tailored suit seemed molded to his slender frame. The man exuded a sense of refined sophistication, yet there was an underlying tension in his posture.

Chelsey rose. "May I help you?"

"I hope so," the man said. "My name is Elliot Saunders."

Nobody reacted except Scout, whose breath hitched.

"*The* Elliot Saunders?" the girl asked.

Lost, LeVar looked from Saunders to the teenager. "What's happening here?"

Scout glanced at LeVar in disbelief. "You can't be serious. Don't you follow the advances in artificial intelligence coming out of Harmon?"

"Uh, should I?"

Raven cleared her throat. "How can we help you, Mr. Saunders?"

Saunders entered the room. "I apologize for the intrusion."

Chelsey motioned for him to take a seat. "Mr. Saunders, to what do we owe this unexpected pleasure?"

Saunders set a folder on her desk, his hand pulling away as if relinquishing something toxic.

"I've come because I'm in trouble."

He opened the folder. LeVar approached to examine its contents: a series of printouts, each dense with text and bearing the anonymity of digital communication. Emails and social media messages. Words slashed across page after page.

"What's the deal with the messages?" LeVar asked.

"Someone has taken a rather intense dislike to my work—or to me personally. The correspondences are becoming worrisome."

A garb of messages carried veiled threats. Against the quiet hum of computer fans, there was a whisper of something dangerous. This was a reminder that technology could be both shield and weapon.

"May we?" LeVar asked, reaching for the folder.

"Please."

"Who sent these?"

"If only I knew."

LeVar considered his options. It was obvious the sender wished Saunders ill, but there wasn't enough here to take the documents to Thomas and get the sheriff's department involved.

"What would you like from us?"

"I want you to find out who sent these messages and stop them before the situation escalates."

"You're a technology expert."

Saunders crossed one leg over the other. "While I know a little about artificial intelligence, I'm not an expert at catching digital ghosts."

Scout perched on the edge of her chair, ready to burst forth. LeVar glanced at Chelsey and Raven, who nodded in unison.

"This is a task for Scout," he said.

Saunders assessed the girl. He didn't seem convinced that a high school student could help him.

Chelsey caught his resistance and offered reassurance.

"Scout's age belies her expertise," she said, her tone brooking no doubt. "She will be our ace in the hole."

Scout's cheeks flushed with pride, but her eyes remained fixed on the documents; she was already dissecting algorithms and IP addresses in her head, sifting through data like a miner panning for gold.

“Okay, you convinced me.”

"We'll take a two-pronged approach. Digital forensics and meticulous background checks. The latter is where the rest of us come in. Raven Hopkins and I have run background checks for years, and we know what to look for. LeVar isn’t just a private investigator; he’s a deputy with the Nightshade County Sheriff’s Department."

Raven clasped her hands on the desk. "Your immediate safety is paramount. We need to consider protective measures for you. Right now."

Saunders lowered his eyes. “Nobody threatened my life. I’m dealing with harassment.”

“This is the way it begins. I mean to stop this person before the situation escalates.”

LeVar pushed aside the box of danishes. "Mr. Saunders, have you considered anyone within your own professional circle who might harbor ill will? A former colleague, perhaps?"

Lines of worry covered Saunders’ brow. "I've wracked my brain, but no one comes to mind. Everyone I've worked with seemed content. You run into problems and get into arguments, but no one ever showed this level of animosity."

Chelsey closed the folder and passed it to Scout for copying. "Your safety and privacy are our priorities. We’ll get to work right away."

Raven, ever the pragmatist, quoted Saunders a price.

"That seems more than fair," the software developer said.

"Excellent. We'll begin immediately."

With the exchange of signatures and handshakes, they sealed the pact. After the firm's financial situation had fallen on hard times, Chelsey named her best friend the co-owner of Wolf Lake Consulting. Together, they'd attracted higher-paying clients and turned the situation around. LeVar knew the Saunders account would place the firm on stable ground.

After the software developer left the office, Chelsey turned to LeVar and the team. "Okay, thoughts?"

"The dude is scared," said LeVar. "He pretended the threat was only digital, but he's looking over his shoulder."

"Rightfully so," Raven said.

In the corner, Scout's eyes locked onto her computer screen.

"Scout?" Chelsey asked. "Will your admiration of Elliot Saunders affect your ability to work?"

The girl set down the mouse. "Never."

"How will you help us find our suspect?"

"Patterns. There will be patterns in the messages. I can find them. Whoever this guy is, he doesn't hide his online presence everywhere. Only when he's threatening Saunders."

"Good. We're going to need your expertise. This stalker knows how to cover his tracks."

"He'll never see me coming."

"Stealth mode. I like it," LeVar said.

The team members shared determined looks. Wolf Lake Consulting's future hung on this investigation.

3

The road unfurled like a ribbon and weaved through the heart of the forest. It led Emma Walsh back to Wolf Lake. Back home.

Behind the wheel, she drove as if outrunning the images that replayed in her mind. Shadows from a nightmare clung to her thoughts. Hannah, lost forever.

Trees stood sentinel along the route. With each turn, the landscape whispered memories and carried her back to a time when laughter echoed through the village and friends shared secrets beneath the stars. She remembered Hannah's grin, the way it lit up her face, how it felt like a promise that nothing could go wrong.

But everything did.

The decision to return had been impulsive—a last-minute use of vacation days that now seemed foolish. With a journalist's instincts and a trail gone cold, what could she hope to accomplish? The lake appeared on her right, its surface a still mirror reflecting a sky too vast to hold answers.

As Wolf Lake emerged, buildings seemed to pop out of the

ground. Branson's Bar, with its neon sign, dared her to revisit days gone by. The playground, where echoes of children's laughter had long since faded, made a lump form in her throat. And the corner store—its windows displaying wares as they had decades ago—beckoned with the allure of a past life.

Her left leg drummed and kept time with the tires bouncing against the pavement. She'd grown up too fast. Now she returned to the place where childhood ended, chasing the ghost of a friend who never received the chance to fulfill her dreams.

The town embodied a living memory. It offered no reprieve from the quest that brought her back—to unearth the truth, to honor a bond that not even time could sever. She had chosen her solitary pursuit solemnly, knowing the cost of looking back and yet unable to do anything else. Her parents had long since moved to Florida to escape the frigid winters of Upstate New York. Dad had high blood pressure, and Mom's skin-and-bones physique made Emma worry.

The Bluewater Tribune appeared on the right. Had she not gotten a huge break after college and landed a writing job in Buffalo, she might have worked here. She passed without slowing. Her presence in Wolf Lake needed no announcement, especially not to a newspaper that prided itself on exploiting others.

A business she didn't recognize popped up in the village center. Wolf Lake Consulting, a private investigative firm. The idea of stopping tempted her. Perhaps she would if the official channels ran dry. But the numbers in her bank account argued louder than desire. She needed to exercise restraint and practicality.

After the commerce thinned out, she found the Nightshade County Sheriff's Department. Her palms dampened on the steering wheel. She imagined walking through those doors unannounced. The story would spill out and meet skepticism.

Or worse, indifference. What kind of man was Sheriff Thomas Shepherd? The car idled as she considered driving off and forgetting this ridiculous idea.

She closed her eyes and saw Hannah. Suddenly, they were twelve years old again.

Hannah shifted her backpack from one shoulder to the other. *"Hey, I have to go down Birch Lane today. Mom needs me to pick up milk on the way home."*

"Want me to come along?"

"Nah, it's fine. Birch is just a quick detour."

Why hadn't Emma followed Hannah to the store? It wasn't out of the way.

Guilt burned in her throat.

She could not leave the story unfinished. For her friend, she would do anything.

The key turned and silenced the car's hum. Panic wrapped stiff fingers around her throat. Her new home in Buffalo was safe, familiar. This was stepping into the abyss. She took a breath. Then another. Time to face the past.

Sunlight glinted against the glass doors of the sheriff's department and hid the faces of those inside. If Sheriff Shepherd wouldn't help, what would she do? Hiring a private investigator would push her to the precipice of bankruptcy.

A child rode past in a winter coat, bundled against the March chill. That could have been her or Hannah a few decades ago.

She entered the building.

~

THE DOOR to Sheriff Thomas Shepherd's office clicked shut, sealing off the outside world. From his desk, Thomas assessed the woman standing in front of him. Lines creased her forehead, but they shouldn't have. This woman couldn't have been older than her late thirties. Her hands trembled, yet her stance spoke of resolve. Who was she, and what did she want from him?

"Emma Walsh," she said. "I'm a reporter . . . No, strike that. I'm a journalist in Buffalo, but I was born and raised in Wolf Lake."

A journalist, not a reporter. Thomas wasn't certain of the difference, but this woman seemed dead set on proving they were different animals.

"How may I help you, Ms. Walsh?"

The story that poured out of the woman made Thomas fidget with a paperweight on his desk. A blue elephant. He didn't even remember where it had come from.

Emma's best friend, Hannah Clarke, had vanished from Wolf Lake in 1998. Thomas recalled the case. He had been six or seven years old when it happened. Mother and Father hadn't allowed him to leave the house for a month.

He set the elephant aside and steepled his fingers. Emma's expression held a plea that needed no words, a silent bargain offered to the universe: attention for answers.

"Tell me about Hannah," he said. His voice carried an unintentional softness; it was the way he'd learned to mask the analytical coldness that often alienated others.

The woman painted a picture of childhood innocence shattered on a spring day when the world turned treacherous. As Emma spoke, he imagined hearing a girl's laughter.

"We were supposed to walk home together. She went to the store. I could have followed, but I didn't."

Thomas noted the quivering lip. He shifted in his chair.

"Twenty-six years is a long time, Ms. Walsh."

His voice was steady, though internally he wrestled with the specter of futility. Cases grew cold, leads turned to dust, and hope often faded into resignation. Sheriff Gray had been in charge back then. Would the former sheriff remember?

"I realize that, but technology allows us to investigate in ways we couldn't have dreamed of during 1998."

Thomas didn't argue. Investigative techniques improved every year. But 1998 was a long time ago.

He looked through the window, past Emma, at the quiet streets of Wolf Lake. Yet he wanted to help. He had to.

"Where do we start?"

The question caught her off guard. The wrinkles of worry vanished, as if smoothed by some mystical ointment.

"You mean you'll help me?"

"That's what I'm here for."

Emma clasped a folder of papers. The edges were worn from handling. She slid it across the desk.

"This is what I've found."

The papers were a collection of notes, interviews, and photographs, a mosaic of new angles on an old tragedy. He picked up the first sheet and scanned the information. A map noted the location where Emma and Hannah had parted ways. The police had spoken to dozens of neighbors between there and the store, and somehow this woman had gotten hold of the documents. She'd also acquired information from a private investigator in Kane Grove, where another girl had vanished that year under similar circumstances. Impressive work. Well, Emma Walsh was a journalist, after all.

"This is thorough."

"In my opinion," Emma said, "Hannah never made it to the store."

"You think the abductor grabbed her before then? It was three o'clock in the afternoon, and people were out."

"This guy has a knack for it."

Has a knack for it? Was she suggesting the predator was still active?

The information was compelling, different from the dead ends that had characterized the initial inquiry. More complete.

He shuffled through more pages, each offering pieces of a puzzle left unsolved for far too long.

While he studied the evidence, she whispered, "Thank you."

He looked up. "For what?"

"For helping me."

Her eyes glistened. Relief and hope flashed in a delicate balance on her face.

"Thank you for bringing this to my attention. I'll need to speak with my deputies. We have a few cases on the docket, but I'll see where we can go from here."

"I appreciate this, Sheriff Shepherd. This means so much."

"Call me Thomas. We're past formalities, I believe."

"Thomas." Her smile held a mixture of gratitude and something akin to camaraderie. "I'll let you get back to work. When can I expect to hear from you?"

"Later today. You'll leave me your number?"

"It's on the folder."

He led her to the door. "You're on a difficult road, but you're not walking it alone anymore."

Emma's hand rested on the doorknob before she stepped into the corridor. Her sneakers squeaked against the mopped floor as she passed Maggie's desk.

He returned to his chair and stared at the wall, seeing not the commendations and certificates but the image of a young girl's face—a girl who had become nothing more than a statistic.

Then he set the folder aside and strode to the storage room. Dust motes floated in the slanting sunlight as he searched the shelves, his fingers eventually landing on a box labeled in faded ink: "Hannah Clarke—1998."

Pulling the box from its resting place, he placed it on a table. Inside lay the remnants of hope suspended in time, waiting for someone like Emma Walsh to challenge the silence. Thomas felt the pull of a new mystery, the call to justice that had led him to wear the badge.

"Let's see what we missed."

4

Chelsey set her feet on the edge of the desk and rocked back in her chair. She spread the Elliot Saunders folder on her lap. Worry gnawed at her. The AI specialist wasn't being straight with them. How could a man of Saunders' stature in the technology community not make his share of enemies?

A motorcycle roared past the window. Someone was showing off on the center boulevard, popping wheelies and revving his engine. She wondered if Thomas or one of his deputies was lying in wait to nab the speeder.

Back to the task at hand. Depending on what her team members uncovered this morning, she might call Saunders and have him return for a followup. This time, maybe he would remember a few enemies he'd trampled. She wondered about Scout, who was on spring break and working at her desk. The teenager admired Saunders. Would that admiration cloud her judgment?

Chelsey stood behind the girl as lines of code scrolled down the screen.

"Anything new?" Chelsey asked.

"I'm using heuristics to compare messages posted on technology forums. This app allows me to input the messages our digital stalker sent to Saunders. If the software discovers similarities between the suspect's writing pattern and those of public posters, it will give us candidates for further inspection."

"Fascinating." Chelsey rolled up her sleeves. It was warm in the office today. "Scout, how long have you followed Elliot Saunders?"

The girl turned around in her chair. "A few years. Why?"

"He's like a technology superstar, right?"

"Sort of. He's certainly a huge name in the northeast, but you won't hear too many conversations about him in Silicon Valley."

"I see." This was good. Scout seemed able to compartmentalize her admiration. "This AI stuff really fascinates you, doesn't it?"

Scout removed her glasses and cleaned them on her shirt. "It will replace online search within five years. I guarantee it."

"Are you saying I should sell my Google stock?"

"Not necessarily. Google has its own AI model, and it is well-funded."

"I'm calling Saunders back to the office," said Chelsey.

"Really?"

"I can't imagine that he hasn't made his fair share of enemies. It seems strange that he didn't recall anybody who wanted to bring him down."

While Scout worked, Chelsey called Raven and LeVar together.

"I'll get the kitchen ready for a roundtable discussion," Raven said.

"Appreciate it."

"And I'll follow up with Harmon PD," LeVar said. "I want to know if there have been incidents close to Saunders' office."

"Smart idea. I like it." Chelsey clapped her hands. "All right, team. I'll contact our artificial intelligence friend and tell him to stop by."

Chelsey made the call and found Saunders willing to drive over within the hour. In the adjacent kitchen, muted clinks and shuffles meant Raven was laying out notepads and laptops. LeVar's voice traveled down the hall. So far, Harmon PD couldn't recall any mysterious loiterers or vandals near the client's office.

At ten in the morning, the door swung open, and Elliot Saunders stepped inside. He wore a windbreaker that was perfect for the 50-degree weather. After the exchange of pleasantries, Chelsey escorted him to the kitchen, where the other team members waited.

Scout brought everyone coffee. Saunders raised his mug in thanks, and the girl blushed.

"Mr. Saunders," Chelsey began, "I'd like to talk about the people you've worked with over the last three years. Anyone stand out as antagonistic?"

Saunders' gaze flitted towards Raven, then away, as if the directness of her stare might strip him of his defenses. His hair blew around as the vents kicked on.

"Antagonistic?" Saunders asked. "No. I consider everyone I've worked beside a colleague. We don't always agree. That's the nature of a fast-moving business. But arguments never get heated. Just the usual back and forth."

"Any unusual exchanges? Anything out of the ordinary that made you wonder about a person's intentions?" Chelsey probed, watching his face for telltale cracks.

Raven leaned back, missing nothing. She read the tension in Saunders' posture.

"Confrontations in the field," LeVar said. "We've all had them. You've had them too, right?"

"Of course. AI isn't universally embraced. Some believe it is dangerous, but those small minds are few and far between."

"Any threats?"

"No. Artificial intelligence isn't the devil. It's a disruptive technology that challenges old norms."

Chelsey took a sip and lowered her mug. "Who feels threatened by your work, Mr. Saunders?"

"All the crazies who want AI banned. But we expect these reactions. Three decades later, there are still people who want the government to eliminate the internet."

The hum of the refrigerator provided a backdrop to the conversation. Saunders sat, fingers laced together on the table, a barrier against the idea that someone wanted to hurt him.

"It's imperative you think hard about this. Anyone who could bear a grudge strong enough to make things personal?"

Saunders' eyes flicked to the window, watching a sparrow dart by. "There are many bright minds in my field. Bright and competitive."

"Competitive how?" Raven asked.

"Arguments at conferences, debates over publications."

"Anyone stand out?" LeVar said.

A pause stretched, filled only by the ticking of a clock on the wall. Saunders' lips parted, then closed.

"Jonathan Kellerman," Saunders said. "We've had our differences."

“Who is Jonathan Kellerman?”

“A fellow developer who believes we're pushing our technology too far and not considering the potential threat against humanity.”

“How would AI threaten the world?” Chelsey asked.

“You ever see *The Terminator*?”

“Sure. Technological advances allow robots to conquer the world.”

“Something like that, but the people who posit these Armageddon theories are usually looking for publicity.”

"Others?"

"Rebecca Lin," Saunders added. "She lost funding to one of my projects last year. We haven't spoken since."

LeVar jotted the name on a notepad and copied Lin's contact information. "Anyone else?"

"No one."

As moments passed, Saunders unfolded his hands and ran them through his hair. He checked his watch and stood.

"If you will excuse me," Saunders said, "I have a conference call in an hour. Thank you for your thoroughness, but I don't believe these messages are coming from my colleagues. Check the internet for the usual conspiracy theorists. Those are the people most likely to hate me."

Saunders agreed to contact the team if anything changed or he received another message. After the door closed, Chelsey turned to her team.

"Thoughts?"

"Kellerman and Lin," Raven said. "Worth looking into."

"Seems too easy," LeVar added.

Chelsey chewed a nail. "I agree, but those are our only leads."

LeVar peered inside the fridge, removed a kombucha, and leaned against the counter, arms crossed. "He's encountered someone with a grudge."

"For certain. But Saunders is holding back. He didn't give us everything."

Raven stood by the window, eyes narrowed in thought. "Names come too late in the game. Feels like he's protecting someone—or himself."

"Or he's scared," Chelsey said.

"Maybe." Raven turned from the window. "Scared or not, someone's playing mind games with him. Could be Kellerman; could be Lin. Or it might be someone he hasn't considered."

"I want to study his work," LeVar said. "Old partnerships, projects. There's more there."

"For sure."

They returned to the office area, where Scout slid in front of her computer and resumed the search. The software was still running comparisons.

"How did your application do?" Chelsey asked.

"Nothing from the heuristic side, but I found bits and pieces elsewhere," Scout said while opening another window. "I looked up the sender of these hate mails. IP addresses masked and rerouted through servers overseas. Whoever this is knows their way around a firewall."

"Can you trace it back?" Raven asked.

"Working on it. It might take time."

"Time we'll give you," Chelsey said. "In the meantime, we'll start with Saunders' old ties. See what shakes loose."

"On it," LeVar said. "I'll pull records on Kellerman and Lin. Anything they touched that Saunders worked on."

"Let's keep it tight and in-house. The less noise, the better."

"Quiet as a church mouse."

"Church mice don't have to deal with encrypted emails," Scout said.

"No, but they know where the free wafers are."

Raven rolled her eyes, and Chelsey snickered. Every topic came back to food when LeVar was in the room.

"Patterns in Saunders' history could give us the why behind these hate mails," Chelsey said. "We need to map out every controversy, every public spat."

"Who he stepped on to get where he is," Raven said.

"Scout, keep at those digital breadcrumbs. I want to know where they lead."

"Will do," Scout said without breaking stride.

LeVar glanced around the room. He stretched, the sound of

popping joints like firecrackers. "Tough night with Aguilar at the gym. I'm hungry. Anyone up for a run to The Broken Yolk?"

"Seriously?" Raven arched an eyebrow. "Thinking with your stomach again?"

"Man's gotta eat." LeVar shrugged, a lopsided grin spreading across his face.

"Sure, and at this rate, you'll eat your way right out of fitting through the door," Chelsey said with a smirk.

"Ha-ha, very funny. But seriously, donuts and bagels could fuel some breakthroughs here."

"Only thing breaking will be the floorboards under your weight," Raven said.

He grabbed his keys. "Keep it up, and I'll come back with only enough for me."

"Like you'd share, anyway."

"Touché."

"All right, fine," Chelsey said. "Get the food. But make it quick. We've got a cyber stalker to catch, and we're not letting your stomach slow us down."

"Roger that. Back in a flash."

5

Sheriff Thomas Shepherd absorbed what Emma had told him. The journalist hadn't stopped by the office since yesterday, but her story remained at the forefront of his mind. What demons haunted her? How could a child process losing her best friend?

He emerged from his office and found Deputies Lambert and Aguilar, the former's arms folded across his chest, the latter tapping a pen against her notepad.

"Quiet around here the last week," Lambert said. The ex-army soldier glanced at the sleepy hum of traffic beyond the windows. "I like it."

"Don't get used to it," said Thomas. He handed Lambert a copy of the case file. "A girl named Hannah Clarke vanished during Sheriff Gray's days. This one dates back to 1998, but I think it's time we took another look."

Aguilar stopped her rhythmic tapping and fixed Thomas with a stare. "That one's been cold for years. Is there recent evidence?"

"The reporter . . . I mean, the journalist who stopped in yesterday is a woman named Emma Walsh. She grew up in Wolf

Lake and has a stake in this. Hannah was her friend. She believes there's more to find, and I agree."

Lambert shifted his weight from one foot to the other. "We're entering the Wayback Machine for this one. But it seems you're set on reopening the case."

"I am."

"Then we're with you," Aguilar said.

"Good. I pulled everything we have on Clarke. There might be something we missed, something new we can test."

"Forensics have come a long way since then."

"But we don't have so much as a hair fiber. The girl just disappeared."

"Guess it's back to the lab for us," Lambert said, a half-smile playing on his lips as opened the folder and paged through the documents.

"Starting at square one."

"Anything Gray can add that might help?"

"The man retired. I'd prefer that he spend his days hunting and fishing. But if it comes to it, I'll make the call."

By noon, remnants of the past covered the table. Photographs, interview transcripts, and forensic reports formed a collage.

"It appears the department canvassed the neighborhood where Clarke disappeared," Lambert said.

"A few people mentioned they noticed the girl passing their houses. No one claims they saw anything out of the ordinary."

"Time alters perspectives. Some might see things in a different light now. Could be worth knocking on a few doors."

"That's what I'm thinking."

"It might be as simple as someone spotting a vehicle in the area around the time she vanished. From the reports, most assumed the kidnapper was a stranger. But what if this guy was a neighbor, someone people trusted?"

Aguilar sipped from a mug of tea. "No one likes to admit their town has skeletons in the closet. I'll dive into the digital side. Back then, we didn't have half the tech we do now. Social media, cloud data—they weren't around in 1998."

"New technologies could turn old ends into beginnings," Thomas said, his mind already sifting through possibilities.

"We can hope."

"Public appeal, then?"

"We could shake the tree, see what falls out." Lambert's tone was light, but his eyes were serious.

"We'll divide and conquer. Aguilar, take the digital. Lambert, you're on the streets."

"Copy that, Thomas."

Thomas looked from one deputy to the next. They were partners in the hunt for truth. "Let's find what's been hiding all these years."

They dispersed, each to a different battleground, armed with resolve and the hope that justice for Hannah Clarke was still within reach. He turned back to the evidence, the silent witnesses of a story left unfinished.

~

Several hours uncovered no new leads. Thomas was frustrated with the lack of progress, but happy to return home. His A-frame, which had belonged to his aunt and uncle during his childhood, stood on the lake shore. The guesthouse where LeVar lived was out back. The guesthouse windows were dark; LeVar must still be in class.

When he entered his house, the excited skitter of paws on floorboards announced that his dog Jack was coming. The massive wolf-like pup bounded toward him, a blur of fur and loyalty. Tigger, the tabby Chelsey had rescued, slinked around his legs.

"Look who showed up," Chelsey called out from the living room, her voice threaded with humor and mock annoyance. She sat amidst a sea of cream paper and ribbon curls, wedding invitations sprawled like confetti around her. They had set the wedding for May. Only two months away. It didn't seem real.

"Sorry about that. Got caught up with an investigation at the office. I promised to help you, didn't I?"

She waved him off with a chuckle, beckoning him closer. "Come here. You've been dodging these for weeks." She patted the couch cushion next to her, a mischievous glint in her eyes.

He hesitated then relented, joining her on the couch. "I was thinking, maybe just family and close friends? Keep it small?"

"Small?" Her eyebrow rose in playful challenge. "Thomas Shepherd, are you suggesting we snub our entire acquaintance list?"

"It wouldn't be a snub. Just keep things intimate."

"Intimate, right." Chelsey leaned back, considering. "I have cousins on my mother's side I haven't seen in decades. If I invite them, will they think we just want a gift?" She rubbed her forehead. "And if I don't invite them, will they feel insulted?"

"All the more reason to keep the list small." He reached for an invitation, turning it over in his hands. "I've been meaning to mention this to you. A woman named Emma Walsh came by the office yesterday."

"Related to an investigation?" Interest piqued, Chelsey turned to him. "What did she want?"

"She wants me to reopen a cold case. It's personal for her. When she was twelve, she was walking home with her friend, Hannah. They split off when Hannah went to the store. Except the girl never made it."

"Abducted?"

"Seems that way. They never found her."

"That's horrible."

Outside the window, blue gloaming reflected off the lake waters.

"What about you guys? What's new at Wolf Lake Consulting?"

"We're trying to catch a cyber stalker. Ever heard of a guy named Elliot Saunders?" she asked.

"Can't say that I have. Is he famous or something?"

She rolled her eyes toward the Mournings' house, which stood next door. "Scout sure thinks so. This Saunders guy is a big deal in the artificial intelligence community. Someone is sending him harassing messages."

"Do the digital footprints lead anywhere?"

"Maybe." She picked at a loose thread on a cushion. "It's a maze, but mazes have exits."

"True. You'll catch the guy like you always do."

"Like you'll find the truth about Hannah Clarke."

"Hope so. Hannah's picture gives me the chills. It's like her ghost is speaking to me."

"Sometimes, it's the old cases that haunt us the most," Chelsey replied, her eyes not leaving his face. "They stick to you."

"It's about giving her family peace. Closure for Emma as well."

"Your tenacity makes you a good sheriff. But remember, it's okay to lean on others. You're still delegating responsibility to Lambert and Aguilar, right?"

"Yeah, but delegating is never easy." A half-smile tugged at his lips. "Not always my strong suit."

"Nor was it mine until I made Raven co-owner of the firm."

Jack trotted into the room, a ball clenched between his teeth,

Tigger hot on his heels. The cat swiped at the dog's tail, eliciting a playful growl.

"Those two," Chelsey said. "They're nothing but mischief."

"Seems they know when to intervene."

She took the ball and tossed it across the room. The dog gave chase.

"About the wedding," she said. "I know you don't like crowds, and this is a lot for you to handle. Let's find a middle ground."

"Middle ground. I can do that."

In the kitchen, pots clanged and the water ran. They moved around each other with an ease borne of familiarity, chopping vegetables and seasoning meat. Laughter mingled with the sizzle of onions in the pan. It was nice to have a sense of normality. Thomas couldn't wait until they were officially married, but imagining all those people, many of which would be strangers, crowding around made him jittery. Why couldn't they just invite Chelsey's parents, his mother, and the investigation teams?

Dinner plates clinked under the scrape of cutlery. She spoke of a mystery she was reading. He wondered why someone who spent every day solving mysteries would bother.

They ate in companionable conversation. Jack didn't beg for treats, but he watched every bite with great interest.

With dinner cleared away, they settled into the evening's lull. Thomas unfolded the papers, the department's letterhead staring back at him, the case file numbers meaningless symbols. His pen hovered, not touching down.

Chelsey lounged on the couch, a cushion propping her up as she opened her book. She lost herself in the pages while he worked.

Thomas tried to read the witness statements, but the words jumbled together, letters scattering like startled birds. Instead, he pictured Hannah Clarke the way Emma described her: young, vibrant, then just gone. The store she'd walked to didn't even exist anymore. An apartment complex stood in its place. He imagined the girl on a street corner, a stranger approaching with the worst intentions.

"Can't concentrate?" Chelsey's voice pulled him out of his head.

"It's haunting." He set the papers aside. "Hannah died, and Emma never had a chance to say goodbye."

"Give it a rest, Thomas," she said, marking her place with a finger. "Tomorrow you can approach the investigation with a fresh perspective."

"I suppose you're right."

He yawned. Maybe she was right about putting the case aside for tonight. They were a team in life and work, bound by more than cases and criminals. The night wrapped around them, quiet and calculating.

But one thought sent a chill down his spine. Was the kidnapper still here in Wolf Lake?

6

The clock ticked past six in the morning, and outside the window, Nightshade County slept under a blanket of fog. In his office, Sheriff Thomas Shepherd spread the Hannah Clarke case files before him. He knew one thing about kidnappers and murderers: They didn't stop until the police caught them. Was their unsub in prison, or was he still hunting the playgrounds and parks for new victims?

He ran a hand through his sandy hair. Hannah had been missing long enough to haunt the town's memory, but not long enough for him to give up hope that justice could prevail.

The front door to the department opened. At first, he thought Maggie was here early. But it was Emma Walsh who stepped inside. He came into the hallway to meet her. Despite the lines of worry around her eyes, her stare mirrored his own determination.

"Morning, Sheriff Shepherd," she said.

"Emma. I didn't expect you to arrive so early."

"I couldn't sleep," she replied, brushing a curl of red hair from her face.

"Since you're here, I should introduce you to my team."

Thomas gestured towards the two deputies who had risen from their desks at her entrance. Lambert's military posture was softened by the hint of a smile. Beside him, Aguilar offered a nod and an unreadable expression. The diminutive deputy had never cared for reporters. Given enough time, she would warm up to Emma.

"Emma Walsh, meet Lambert and Aguilar."

"Ms. Walsh," Lambert extended a hand, his grasp firm. "Thomas mentioned you yesterday."

"Please, call me Emma." She shook his hand, then Aguilar's.

"Emma here is going to help us with Hannah's case," Thomas said. “They were best friends.”

"I’m sorry for your loss," Aguilar said. "All morning, I’ve been looking into similar incidents. These are cold cases I dug through. Take a look."

The files landed on the table with a thud. So many. Thomas blew out a breath.

"Notice anything interesting?" Thomas asked.

“There was a string of kidnappings that extended beyond Nightshade County. Some occurred as far away as Albany and Buffalo.”

“Victimology?”

“Same age range,” Aguilar pointed out, tapping a page. “All girls.”

"Can't be a coincidence."

Appearing stunned, Emma sank into a chair. “I found a handful of missing girls who reminded me of Hannah. But this . . . there must be a dozen kids in that stack.”

Aguilar’s mouth twisted. “More.”

Thomas opened the file on top. "Same age as Hannah."

"Each one. They all range from eleven to fourteen years."

Lambert crossed his arms, the fabric of his shirt stretching over his biceps. "Seems our perp has a type."

"He goes after girls just stepping into their lives," Aguilar said.

"Let's not get ahead of ourselves," said Thomas. "We need more information. This looks like the same guy, but we need to be sure."

Lambert thumbed through another folder. "Time to cast a wider net. You mind if I reach out to other counties?"

"Not at all. I want to speak with any longtime law enforcement officers who were on the job during these investigations."

Lambert returned to his desk and lifted the phone. His voice carried across the station. "Bill, it's Lambert. We need to talk about some cases. Old ones with missing girls."

"Jurisdictions nearby might have run their own profiles," Aguilar said to Thomas, leaning on her elbows.

"If the other counties will work with us, we'll stand a better chance of catching this guy. That is, if he's still loose. He could be dead or imprisoned."

Emma's head turned from Thomas to Aguilar as they traded ideas. "What I noticed is the kidnappings stopped over a decade ago. You might be correct."

Lambert's call continued in the background.

"Work with my deputies, and give them everything you've gathered," Thomas said, looking at Emma. "When we find the pattern, we'll catch the perpetrator."

"Got a bite," Lambert announced, cradling the receiver between his shoulder and ear. "Montrose County has files to share."

"See?" Thomas said. "We're already moving forward."

Dawn filtered through the blinds of the station as Deputy Aguilar arranged the cold case files on the table. Her pen scratched a steady rhythm on a notepad. Bullet points formed the skeleton of what would soon be one comprehensive file.

"What do you see?" Thomas asked.

"Besides the victimology, there is consistency here."

"Consistency is good," Emma said, peering at Aguilar's notepad.

Aguilar stuck pins on a map to mark each missing girl.

"We're dealing with a calculating predator," Thomas said.

"Speaking of calculations," Lambert cut in, settling the phone back into its cradle. "Got word from three counties over. Similar case, matching profile. Another one beyond state lines."

"Cross-state," Thomas said. "That means we're looking at someone who knows how to disappear. Someone meticulous. Law enforcement has become increasingly national, but back in the day, most databases were state-based. It made it easy for serial kidnappers to jump from state to state and avoid detection."

Emma clasped her hands together. “Why didn’t the FBI get involved?”

“Because the states didn’t ask. Until someone saw the pattern, there was no way for the feds to know what was happening. And then there are jurisdictional battles. Some counties and police departments don’t want the FBI poking its nose into their business.”

"This guy was busy," Lambert said. "Once we combine the cases I found with Aguilar’s, we’ll have eighteen or twenty on our hands."

"A serial abductor," Aguilar said.

"There’s no doubt."

Thomas paced the length of the room, his back injury a mere ghost in his stride. "He took a few every year. Then the activity stopped."

“Hopefully, he kicked the bucket and isn’t a problem anymore,” Lambert said, his hand instinctively reaching to the back of his neck, as if searching for his military dog tags.

"Let's start by overlaying timelines with geographic patterns," Aguilar suggested, tapping the map.

"Overlay away," Thomas said.

After resetting the pins, Aguilar rubbed her chin. "He was most active between Wolf Lake, Kane Grove, and Montrose County during the late nineties."

Emma rolled a shiver out of her shoulders.

"Then," Aguilar continued, "the pattern shifted south toward the NY and PA border."

"Could be that he moved," said Emma.

"More likely, he changed his routine to throw off law enforcement."

Emma stood opposite Thomas. Her eyes danced between the photographs of the missing girls and Aguilar's notes. "Have we looked at the victims' hobbies and routines? Maybe our guy has a type beyond age and looks."

"School records, sports or clubs," Thomas said. "Aguilar, can you pull that up?"

"Already on it." She punched the information into the computer. "Emma, was Hannah involved in any clubs?"

The journalist scuffed the floor with the toe of her sneaker. "Not really. She stayed active—we were always on our bikes—but she wasn't an athlete. Neither was I."

While Aguilar worked, Thomas propped himself on the corner of the desk. "I realize 1998 was a long time ago—"

"Not for me, it wasn't."

"Understood, but I need you to think back. Was there ever a stranger or a person around town who gave you the creeps?"

She rubbed the goosebumps off her arms. "There was one guy."

"Give me a name. Maybe it will ring a bell."

"Mr. Trevino."

Thomas sifted through the names cataloged in his memory. "Nolan Trevino?"

"Yes, that's him."

"He was an odd fellow, no question. Trevino lived three blocks from where I grew up." Thomas made it a point to not refer to their house as *their estate*. By then, his father had grown Shepherd Systems into a regional powerhouse. "If you ask me, he was harmless. I believe he was on the spectrum like me, but doctors weren't as quick to diagnose autism and Asperger's back then."

Emma appeared flabbergasted. "You're on the spectrum?"

"I am."

"I never would have guessed."

"Well, thank you. Anyway, Trevino died some time back."

"How far back?" Lambert asked as he took a seat beside them.

"About ten years ago." Thomas's eyes narrowed. "Hold on."

There was no reason for him to believe Nolan Trevino would have harmed a child, but he didn't like coincidences. A few keystrokes and mouse clicks got him into the country records.

"Died in 2012," Thomas said.

Aguilar joined them. "Right around the time the kidnappings stopped."

He rocked back in his chair. "No, I refuse to believe Nolan Trevino is our kidnapper."

"Emma says he watched her in the park, and the timeline matches."

"Come on. There isn't a shred of evidence pointing to this guy. The last thing Trevino would do is hurt a kid."

No, it had to be someone else.

7

Whoever this guy was, he was good. Scout couldn't pin him down.

At her desk inside Wolf Lake Consulting, the teenager checked the lines of code cascading down the screen, a digital waterfall of information that seemed to mock her with its complexity. Saunders' stalker was proving to be a master of digital disguise.

Her glasses caught the light; behind them, the dance of data flickered in her eyes.

LeVar leaned against the doorframe, arms crossed as he watched Scout's battle with the elusive prey. "You'll nail him. Ain't nobody better at this than you."

She glanced at him, the corner of her mouth twitching up despite her clear frustration. "This one plays hard to get." But there was a reluctant respect in her words. To evade her like this, the stalker had to have skills.

"Hard to get means worth the chase," LeVar replied, pushing off from the frame and stepping closer. His dreadlocks swayed with the movement. "At least that's what I told myself every time a shorty jilted me back in the day."

A blush crept into Scout's cheeks. "I'm not sure how to use that information."

"Keep at it. You're gonna crack this code."

Chelsey and Raven entered the office carrying smoothies they'd concocted in the kitchen. Chelsey slid into her chair at the desk beside Scout's. Raven sat across from them.

"Saunders' assets," Raven said. "We've tallied it up. The man's sitting on a mountain of cash."

"Millions," Chelsey said. "Millions that could tempt even the most reclusive hacker out of hiding."

Scout had figured Saunders was wealthy, but not to this degree. Murmurs rippled through the room. "Money like that is a beacon. But it's only going to grow. If Saunders goes public with his AI tech, his wealth will explode."

"An IPO?" Chelsey asked. "That's not just a beacon. It's a freaking lighthouse."

"It paints an even bigger target on his back."

The office fell silent as they considered the implications. A fortune that could swell overnight was motive enough for any crime, let alone cyber stalking. But the question lingered: Was money the root or a branch of something more twisted?

Raven reached for her phone, pressed a few buttons, and set it down. The speaker engaged with a soft beep and filled the room with its electronic hum.

"Are you calling Saunders?" Chelsey asked.

"Yep," Raven said. "I told him we'd check in this morning. Should I ask him about a potential IPO?"

"He might balk at sharing that information."

The phone started ringing.

"Saunders here," came the voice.

"Mr. Saunders, this is Raven Hopkins checking in. We're all here."

"Progress?" There was a hint of impatience in his tone.

"We're closing in on a handful of IP addresses and piecing things together."

"Good to hear. I want this guy to stop harassing me," he said.

"Has there been any contact in the last twenty-four hours?"

"No, but he's due."

"Your finances," Chelsey said. "They're extensive and growing."

"Part of the game," Saunders said with a chuckle.

"Which makes you a target," LeVar said.

"I don't believe this guy wants my money. It's hate, plain and simple. He doesn't approve of the progress I'm making. At least the threat is digital and not physical."

"Digital threats escalate," Raven said. "Vigilance is key."

"Yeah, I suppose. Appreciate the hard work, but I don't want to deal with the messages anymore. I have a business to run and can't afford distractions."

The call ended with a click, and the team sat in silence. Scout chewed the inside of her cheek. She admired Saunders, but pulling back the curtain had revealed a man who could be difficult.

Raven leaned forward, her braids shifting like dark ropes over her shoulders. "Online can turn offline in a hurry. I have a sick feeling that this stalker will go after Saunders."

"Scout, are the messages becoming more threatening?" Chelsey asked.

The girl picked at a piece of invisible lint on her skirt. What if she missed an important piece of information? She could be the reason Saunders never saw his enemy coming. As much as she wanted to work for the FBI someday, she was beginning to understand the immense pressure that came with the job.

"No, but the frequency is increasing."

LeVar glanced at the clock. "I gotta head out. There's a

lecture on criminal psychology at the college. I'm required to attend."

Her shoulders slumped. When the pressure mounted, LeVar always kept her grounded. Now she felt alone.

"Catch you later at your place?" she asked.

"Sounds good. I'll hit you with a text when I leave."

LeVar grabbed his jacket.

"Cool."

The door clicked shut behind him, leaving Scout alone with her digital puzzle. Chelsey conferred with Raven. They were discussing security logistics, but Scout couldn't hear what they said. The room seemed to shrink as she focused all her attention on the pixels dancing under her eyes.

Scout kept searching. Once, she'd caught a serial killer by using these techniques. But this guy was tougher. He knew his way around the digital landscape. Even better than she did.

"Can I get you a coffee?" Chelsey asked.

"No, thank you. I'm good," Scout said. "Anyhow, I don't want to ruin my train of thought."

"You've been at it for over two hours. It's good to take a break."

She would, but not yet.

As Scout ran another search on the stalker's messages, Raven followed Chelsey into the kitchen. Now she really was on her own.

The wind gusted against the old, converted house and rattled the windows. Outside, a woman lowered her head, pulled her coat together, and hurried to the car. The weather reminded Scout of how cruel the end of March could be in Wolf Lake. Everyone was thinking spring, but winter refused to give up the fight. She turned her attention to the monitor.

There it was. A disturbance in the pattern, the ghost of an anomaly bearing secrets. Scout leaned in, her chest tight with anticipation. It was subtle, almost imperceptible, but to her trained eye, it sang of possibility. Maybe this stalker wasn't perfect after all. The data told her where the message had come from—Syracuse. It was a start.

"I see you," she whispered with a small smile. The thrill of the chase surged through her.

She turned to tell LeVar about her progress before she remembered he was gone.

8

Clara and James Hartley were somewhere north of Wolf Lake, driving down a road marked by nothing but encroaching forest. Branches hanging over the macadam swayed in the window, and every blacktop shadow seemed like a beast crawling out of the ground. The Tears for Fears song on the radio put Clara in a nostalgic state. She remembered the way she'd styled her hair in a high-side ponytail while she courted James. That must have been thirty years ago, and here they were, six months from their twentieth wedding anniversary.

"Where are we?" she asked.

"Halfway between Treman Mills and Wolf Lake, if I had to guess."

"Please tell me you aren't guessing."

"I'm pretty sure I know where we are."

Pretty sure? She hoped the lake would appear on the other side of this forest, which seemed to stretch forever. Maybe they weren't as close to Wolf Lake as he believed.

"James, if you want to use the GPS—"

A deafening pop. Then the nails-on-chalkboard squeal of

the car skidding across the pavement at 45 mph. She grabbed the door handle and held her breath as he turned into the skid, then back again, until the car stopped on the shoulder. A cloud of dusty gravel rained down on the windshield.

"Are you all right?" he asked, touching her hand.

"Just a little shaken up. Thank God the car didn't flip."

He didn't reply, but she could see the same thought haunting his eyes.

When his door opened, she joined him on the shoulder. "Now what?"

"I guess I should change the tire."

"When was the last time you changed a flat?"

He ran a shaky hand through his hair. "Pop showed me when I got my learner's permit."

"James, you were, like, sixteen."

"I remember, I swear."

He popped the trunk and pushed aside a myriad of jumbled items: two yellow ponchos, charging cables, several magazines she'd meant to toss in the recycling bin, and what appeared to be melted candy. She helped him clear enough space for him to open the compartment.

The stench of rubber reached her nose and made her feel a little sick to her stomach. There was the spare. That was a start.

He wrestled with the tire until it came free. "Dammit, where is the jack?"

"I see the lug wrench. Want me to remove the wheel?"

"Let me do it, Clara. You're cold."

"No, I'm not."

"Have you ever removed a tire before?"

She hadn't. So much for independence. As much as she hated to admit it, she still relied on him when something like this happened. Her own father had taught her to change a tire, but she couldn't remember. But was James better prepared than her?

Clara wrapped her arms around herself and bounced on her heels. The snow had melted weeks ago, but it didn't feel like spring. Not with the wind numbing her fingers and searching for a way inside her clothes. She glanced down the road, hoping someone would come around the bend and help. How would James react if he needed someone to get them out of this mess?

He was still looking for the jack as she checked her phone. No bars. The couple exchanged a look. With no cell service to call for help and the nearest town miles away, they were in trouble.

"Ah, here it is," he said.

When he lifted the jack out of its compartment, she felt a modicum of hope. He kneeled beside the flat. She paced up and down the shoulder praying for bars, as he grunted and strained to remove the lug nuts. Ten minutes passed, and he'd only removed three.

"Why don't you take a break and let me help?"

"I got it, Clara. It's this one nut. Stupid thing corroded. I'm afraid to strip it."

"Don't worry about stripping it. It's not even moving."

"It will. I just need to catch my breath."

She hoped he wouldn't throw out his back fighting with the blown tire. Last year, he'd wrenched his back by falling on the ice. It had taken three months for him to recover.

Despite his persistence, the nut wouldn't budge, not even with both of them putting their weight on the wrench and pushing down.

They collapsed against the car and sat panting.

"You're right," he said. "I need professional tools to remove this tire."

"Are you sure Wolf Lake is a few miles down the road?"

He closed his eyes and knocked the back of his head against the door. “No.”

Well, he’d finally admitted the truth. They were lost. No sense in following the road if it led to nowhere.

“A driver will come past. Be ready to flag him down.”

“No service on my phone, either.” He stood and touched his lower back. Surveying the landscape, he pointed at the rising terrain on one side of the road. “If we climb, we should find a signal.”

“It’s worth a try.”

Anything was better than sitting here, waiting for help that might never arrive. One positive—it was still early afternoon. They had enough daylight to work with. If it had been dusk . . .

She shivered at the thought.

James reached down and clasped her hand. She didn’t want him to test his back by helping her stand, but he needed to be the protector. Hell, she *needed him* to be the protector.

Across the road was a stand of trees that revealed only blackness beyond their gangling limbs. Venturing forth felt like a terrible idea. What choice did they have?

The March chill wrapped around her body. Now the wind gusted from behind, shoving her forward, as if it conspired with the dark maw of the woods.

Stepping into the forest made her flesh prick. They picked their way around the trees, their breaths labored as they started up the incline.

"James, the footing isn’t stable. I don't like this."

"Let's get up this hill. I’m positive we'll find a spot with cell service once we're higher up."

As they climbed, the dark became oppressive. This was an alien world.

Yet a hint of brightness above urged her to struggle on. Was that a clearing? A vague trail marked the way forward, proof that someone had come this way. Hunting season was a long way off, but that didn't stop people from killing game when law enforcement wasn't watching.

The trees parted, and they stepped into a clearing. Thank goodness they'd reached the top. Clara scanned the area for signs of civilization, but she only saw more trees pressing against the clearing's perimeter. The footpath continued here. Matted grass and muddy boot prints made her worry that they weren't alone.

"What in the hell?"

She turned toward his voice. Several crude crosses made of sticks jutted out of the ground.

"James, what do you think those are?" Her imagination ran wild with horrific possibilities. "Why would anyone put those here?"

"Could be an old pet graveyard. I wouldn't fret over it."

Yet she couldn't help but worry. This was wrong. An abomination.

"Nobody owns this land. Why would there be a pet graveyard?"

"Those crosses could be anything. Maybe they mark a local hiking trail, or someone set up a memorial for a loved one. There's no reason to jump to conclusions."

He squeezed her hand, but the gesture failed to calm her racing thoughts.

"This isn't a hiking trail, and I can't imagine anyone memorializing a loved one in the middle of nowhere."

"Just keep going," he said, reaching out to take her hand. "We came here to check for a signal, right?"

He was right. She checked her phone and found a bar. Only one, but it might be enough.

She dialed the sheriff's station and braced herself when the phone rang. Then it cut off.

"I almost had it, James."

"I'll try next." He got the same result. "The village of Wolf Lake is that way."

She looked past his outstretched arm. "Down the other side of the hill?"

"I think so. The problem is, the wind is at our backs. If it turns around, we should get a better signal. Keep trying."

A limb crackled out of sight. Her eyes darted around the woods.

"Nobody should be out here," she said.

"I didn't hear anyone."

As she rechecked her phone, footsteps crunched through the underbrush. It wasn't from the direction they had come; it was from ahead.

"There's someone out there, James."

"Good. They can help us get back on the road."

A sound traveled on the wind. It could have been an animal. Yet it sounded like chuckling. Someone was watching.

The blood drained from James's face.

"Did you hear that?" Clara asked.

His grip on her hand tightened. "Yeah, I heard it too."

The footsteps grew closer, the sound echoing through the trees in a sinister heartbeat. Panic clawed at her throat.

"Hello?" he called.

She covered his mouth. "Don't. What if it's a person up to no good?"

"We can't assume the worst."

"Why can't we? Better safe than sorry."

The click of a gun cocking shattered the rest of his bravado. "Run."

They hurried out of the clearing as the footsteps gained on them. He still had a hold of her wrist as they clambered down the hill, retracing their steps. Now she wanted to see the road, to see signs that humanity had once been here.

She couldn't tell if the footsteps were chasing them. Dead leaves crumbled under their shoes as they skidded and stumbled down the decline. Was the car this way? How could she be certain?

"James, where are we going? We're getting lost."

"Keep running. We'll worry about where we are after."

The farther she ran, the more disoriented she became. The forest blended together into an indistinguishable mass.

At last, he stopped, supported himself against a tree and squinted through the gloom. "We have to catch our breath."

She searched for a familiar landmark and found nothing. Sinking behind the oak tree, she let her racing pulse slow down. Gnarled roots offered a semblance of shelter. Sweat dripped from her brow. "Do you think we lost him? Whoever it was?"

"I don't hear him anymore. Stay quiet and wait a little longer. We need to be sure."

Who was following them? And how had a simple search for a signal turned into a terrifying game of cat and mouse?

That chuckling sound came again from up the hillside.

"He's still out there."

"Stay here," he said. "I need to get a look at who's following us."

"Don't."

"If I can't see him, he can't see me. Promise you won't move from this spot."

Before she could argue, he crept away.

~

HE WATCHED them from the shadows. Mud squelched underfoot as he shifted in his crouch. They had seen too much.

Peering out from behind a tree, he observed their frenzied prints in the soft earth. As the impressions continued down the hill, the ground hardened where the dense canopy shielded the forest floor from rainfall. This made it more difficult to track their footprints.

But he could see the couple. The man had broken off from the woman, as if meaning to confront him. The figure pocketed his gun and removed a hunting knife from its sheath.

"Come out, come out, wherever you are," he sang.

The man and woman had found his crosses. So they needed to die.

He berated himself for not being more careful. How could he have predicted their car would break down at the base of the hill, or that they'd hike to the clearing? *His* clearing. He couldn't allow them to escape.

A rustling in the brush caught his attention. He held his breath, waiting for the sound to repeat itself. Was the man close?

The killer stepped out from behind the tree. His secret must remain hidden.

9

The guest house smelled like sauce—a sweet and savory Italian sauce, laced with herbs and a hint of roasted peppers. Scout guessed that LeVar was making pizza.

The clouds had broken up and allowed a little late day sun to bathe Wolf Lake. But even with the sun, the temperature was too cool. It wasn't time to forget jackets and think about shorts. Maybe in a month or two, but not yet.

She rapped on LeVar's door and waited, jogging in place to warm up. In the crook of one arm lay a laptop. He pulled back the curtain, recognized her, and grinned.

"You're just in time," he said, padding to the kitchenette while she set down the laptop on the card table inside the front room. "I was gonna order a pie from the Wolf Lake Bakery. Then I thought, why don't I make one myself? I know what I want on my pizza better than any restaurant does."

"I can't argue with your expertise."

"Are you saying I eat a lot of pizza, Scout?"

"Well, duh."

She couldn't help but giggle when he entered the guest room in a chef's coat. He pointed a sauce-covered spoon at her.

"If y'all diss my eating habits like Raven does, you don't get no pie."

"I'm kidding."

"That's better."

Scout opened the laptop and waited while the computer connected to his Wi-Fi. "How was the speech?"

"At the community college? It was *aight*, I guess. Would have been better off hanging with you guys at WLC and solving the case."

"Which is why I'm here."

"I figured you just wanted dinner."

"LeVar, *you* are the one who's always thinking about food."

"As if you'll turn down a slice."

"Or three?"

"Fine."

Before they worked, he plated dinner in the center of the card table, which wobbled because of one wonky leg. One of these days, she would pool money with their investigating team and buy him a proper table. Except the room barely held a couch, one desktop PC, and the card table.

She checked the crust before taking the first bite. "This is amazing. How did you learn to make New York-style crust?"

"I got mad skills."

"Admit it. This isn't your first attempt."

"Do I have *perfect* tattooed across my forehead? I might have singed a crust or two."

"What became of those pizzas?"

"Most went in the garbage. I gave a few slices to Jack. He's not a pizza snob."

"Not like you."

"Exact-a-mundo, Potsie."

She dabbed a napkin against the corner of her mouth. "Now you're quoting *Happy Days*?"

"Shoulda grown up in the seventies and eighties. They had the best TV shows, the best music. Run DMC and Public Enemy."

"I've heard you singing along to The Smiths."

He paused mid-chew. "That wasn't me."

"LeVar, you have a beautiful voice. You're not quite Morrissey, but I like it."

"Uh . . . well . . . I think you just heard me blasting music and thought it was me singing."

"If you say so."

Scout cherished these moments. Just the two of them, poking fun, enjoying a light conversation, and eating. When they were together, she didn't have a care in the world. He understood her better than Liz, her ghost-hunting friend, or any of the other girls at school. Were all college guys cool and mature like LeVar? All the more reason to graduate early and put high school in the rearview mirror. And truth be told, he made a helluva pizza.

By the time the clock hit six, she'd stuffed her belly. But it was the yummy kind of stuffed that made her crave another slice. She didn't partake. No sense in blowing up three dress sizes with summer on the horizon. Ah, summer. She couldn't wait for vacation, swimming, jogging, and hanging out with LeVar every day. The longing made her cringe at returning to school Monday morning.

He joined her at the window, which looked out at the water. A brave fisher cast a line into the center of the lake as the wind drove waves against the hull. The man had to be freezing.

"Cool that we still have more than an hour until the sun sets," he said. "Daylight savings time is the bomb diggity."

"Sure is. Isn't it depressing when the sun goes down around four o'clock in December?"

"Tell me about it. Now we just need the weather to warm up, and we'll be ready to rock." He elbowed her. "You carried that laptop all the way over here. What's on the docket?"

She brushed her hair with her fingers and returned to the card table. "I thought we could go over what I found at Wolf Lake Consulting."

"Are you homing in on our stalker dude?"

"You'd better believe it. Check it out." Scout opened the laptop and loaded the data she'd gathered earlier.

He tidied up by wiping the table with a wet paper towel. "What am I looking at?"

"I tracked the stalker's IP address. Using a combination of data analysis and some creative digital footwork, I narrowed his location to near Syracuse."

LeVar, his curiosity piqued, abandoned his cleanup efforts and focused on the laptop. "Syracuse, huh? That's a pretty size-able area. How'd you pinpoint it so closely?"

"With a lot of patience and a bit of luck. I cross-referenced the IP addresses with known public Wi-Fi spots, then analyzed the timing and frequency of his online activities. It seems like our guy has a routine, and that routine includes hitting up certain spots around Syracuse and Harmon."

Impressed, LeVar scratched his stubbled cheeks. "That's some serious detective work, Scout. What's the next step? How do we go from 'somewhere near Syracuse' to an actual address?"

"That's where it gets tricky. We need to cross-reference this information with posts this guy made under different pseudonyms."

"Like on forums?"

"Definitely. I can't imagine this stalker's only activity is sending hate messages to Elliot Saunders. If he despises artificial intelligence, he must be voicing his opinions elsewhere."

"Makes sense."

"If we discover overlaps in the location data, we'll pinpoint where this stalker is operating from."

LeVar wiped his hands on his pants. "Looks like we've got our work cut out for us. But hey, if anyone can crack this, it's you."

She couldn't help but feel a rush of pride at his words. "I learned from the best."

"Yeah, Chelsey is the real deal."

"She is. But I meant you, LeVar."

He coughed into his hand and tossed the paper towel in the trash. "You're the computer whiz, my girl. Not me."

"Stop selling yourself short. I can't tell you how much I've learned from you."

As he bagged the trash, he seemed uncomfortable. Had she been too effusive with her praise? She hoped he hadn't interpreted her words as flirting.

"Back to work," he said. "How do we find these pseudonyms he's using?"

"First up, we'll use NLP."

"NLP?"

"Natural language processing tools. NLP can dissect the stalker's messages, breaking them down into identifiable linguistic features. It's like a digital fingerprint of his writing style."

"No kidding? It can really pick out our guy from a sea of internet trolls?"

"Yeah, and we'll find the bridge he's hiding under." Scout launched a software program designed for authorship attribution. "We feed it samples of the stalker's known messages and the program analyzes everything from word frequency to syntactic patterns. Then we do the same with posts from forums and blogs."

Graphs and tables populated the laptop screen, each representing distinct elements of the stalker's writing style. LeVar was too stunned to talk. She navigated the program, setting up parameters for the machine learning model they would use to sift through online posts.

"Now for the heuristic analysis," Scout continued, opening another application. "This will help us narrow our search. We're looking for posts that match specific criteria related to his known interests and patterns of behavior."

LeVar watched, fascinated, as Scout outlined the heuristic rules they would apply. "And if a post hits enough of our criteria, it gets flagged for closer review."

"Right. Every lead is worth investigating."

“Bring this stuff to Chelsey and Raven. Do you realize how this could revolutionize private investigation?”

“I will.”

With the preparatory work done, Scout initiated the scanning process. The laptop crawled through forums and blogs, analyzing a mountain of posts against their database of the stalker's messages. The software flagged each potential match and a list of suspects formed, though none was conclusive.

As the software worked, Scout said, "Once we have a list of potential matches, we'll do a deeper analysis. We'll look at the context of the posts, any recurring themes, and how they might relate to Saunders and his work."

"And we’ll cross-reference everything with locations near Syracuse and Harmon. It's like assembling a giant puzzle."

"It's meticulous work, but every piece brings us closer to the picture we're trying to complete."

For the next hour, they watched as the software filtered through the digital noise of the internet. Outside, the sky darkened and people headed inside. She couldn't wait until this was her everyday job. The longer she sifted through the data, the smaller high school seemed.

Each flagged post was a thread in the vast web of online interactions, a potential lead that could take them closer to their elusive target.

"We might not find him tonight," Scout finally said, stretching her arms. "But we're laying the groundwork."

LeVar, though disappointed, understood the complexity of their task. "Rome wasn't built in a day."

“Nor was it burned to the ground overnight.”

He gestured at the window. “Your mom will wonder where you are. I should take you home.”

“You don't have to.”

He gave her a level look. “Scout, I'm not letting you walk home in the dark with a weirdo watching Saunders.”

“I literally live next door.”

“Even so, it wouldn't be right.”

She groaned. “I guess you're right. Do you mind if the program runs all evening?”

“Nah. Leave your laptop.”

“And hit me with a text if it catches our target.”

“We both need to sleep. All work and no play makes Jack a dull boy.”

“*The Shining*, 1980. Oh, wait. The book came out in 1977.”

He chuckled. “The saying dates back to the seventeenth century.”

“For real?”

“Yeah, for real. See, I learned a few things in college.” He pulled a sweatshirt over his head. “Come on, girl. I'll walk you back.”

10

"We've exhausted our resources," Thomas said.

Standing against the wall inside the sheriff's department, he scratched the back of his head and waited for his deputies to feed him ideas. After calling every sheriff's office and police department in the surrounding counties, he'd given up hope of figuring out who had abducted Hannah and the other girls. In his heart, he hoped the killer was dead and no longer a threat to society. That would explain why the kidnappings had stopped. But he knew better than to assume the terror was over.

"What if we return to the scene of each abduction and interview everyone within a three-block radius?" Aguilar asked.

"Tell me what you're thinking."

"We could catalog everything and search for overlap. A vehicle spotted in the vicinity, a stranger people noticed but thought nothing of. All we need is one matching description."

"I like it. Lambert, what do you say?"

The lanky deputy rolled a knot out of his shoulders. "Aguilar makes sense."

"Darn right," she said, elbowing Lambert hard enough to make him wince.

"Hey, that was a compliment."

"But you made it sound like I rarely make sense."

"Focus," Thomas said. He enjoyed their banter, but now wasn't the time. "I need more ideas." Thomas turned his gaze to the rest of the room, observing every junior deputy present. "We're not just looking for a needle in a haystack; we're trying to find a needle that doesn't want to be found. Every idea counts, no matter how small."

Aguilar cracked her knuckles. "Have we considered using social media and local news to request help from the public? Someone might have seen something but didn't realize its significance."

"There was no such thing as social media when Hannah disappeared."

"No, but everyone remembers missing kids. People might have set up pages dedicated to each missing child."

"That's a thought. I'll put it on my list. We'll draft a press release and a social media appeal. Be specific about what we're looking for—times and locations of each abduction, descriptions of every child. The more eyes we have on this, the better."

"I'll work on the press release with our reporter friend," Lambert said, cocking his head toward Emma, who was working in the far corner of the office.

"Perfect. We also need to dive deeper into the victims' backgrounds. There has to be a connection we're missing. Friends, relatives, hobbies—anything that ties them together."

Aguilar frowned. "Too bad cell phones weren't a thing back then. We could have gotten warrants for the victims' phone records and checked for common numbers or locations pinging at the times of their disappearances."

"Wishes won't get us anywhere."

"All right. How about if we look into more child predators serving time? I realize we searched the surrounding counties. What if we expanded the search to prisons within five hundred miles of Wolf Lake?"

"That's a lot of prison records to check," said Thomas.

"Then we had better start now."

He paused, looking around the room once more. "This is a multifaceted approach. We're going back to the abduction scenes, reviewing footage, engaging the public, analyzing victims' lives, and tracking digital footprints. If we're lucky, we'll get a hit in the prison system and verify that this guy is behind bars forever."

"We still need closure for the victims' families," Lambert said.

"Without question. Until we get a confession and find out where he buried the bodies, we can't help with the grieving processes." The room filled with a renewed sense of purpose. Thomas could see the determination in his teammates' eyes. "We'll catch this guy. I don't doubt that we will."

As the deputies dispersed to their tasks, Thomas stayed back for a moment. He needed to control his emotions. His deputies were doing their best, and no new abductions fit Hannah's profile. So why did he sense they were running out of time?

At Lambert's desk, the deputy worked with Emma. Thomas could see the journalist's head bob in agreement as they shared ideas about what to include in the press release.

In the meantime, Aguilar waded through prison database after prison database. She sent the results to his computer. As they appeared on the screen, he felt hope slipping away. So many names, and she was only a quarter of the way through her search. The number of kidnappers and child murderers serving time sickened him. What was wrong with the world?

Taking half of the search off her hands, he worked through

more of the database. At that moment, a junior deputy with a boyish face burst into the office.

"Sorry to disturb you, Sheriff," the deputy said.

"No need to apologize. What do you have for me?"

"Caller on the line. We have a stranded couple ten miles outside of Wolf Lake."

"Did you tell them to contact a tow company?"

"They tried, but everyone keeps telling them that they're at the back of a long queue. If you ask me, those towing companies are just making excuses because they don't want to drive that far into the country."

"Are these people injured or in trouble?"

"Negative."

Thomas exhaled. "All right. Put them through to my line."

"Will do, Sheriff."

He wished the junior deputies would call him Thomas like everyone else did. Oh well. The new officers would grow more comfortable as time passed and they gained confidence.

Thomas walked to the open door and peeked his head out. "Lambert, could I get your help?"

The senior deputy looked up. "Sure. What's up, Thomas?"

"I've got a stranded couple on hold. Might need you to take care of them."

"I haven't completed the press release."

"That's all right. Have Emma put the finishing touches on the release. I'll check it over afterward."

Lambert conferred with Emma, who appeared ready to take charge. After Lambert joined Thomas in his office, they took chairs on opposite sides of the desk. Thomas clicked the blinking button.

"Sheriff Shepherd and Deputy Lambert here."

The callers identified themselves as Clara and James Hartley.

They were about ten miles outside of Wolf Lake, but neither was sure of their exact location.

"I thought we were on CR-12," James said. "But I took a wrong turn and ended up in the middle of nowhere. The tire blew."

"I trust you didn't wreck the vehicle."

"No, I brought it safely to the shoulder, thank goodness."

"You were fortunate."

"You don't have to tell me. I'm still thanking my lucky stars. Trouble is, I couldn't remove the tire. The lug nuts fused on to the bolts, and the towing companies won't give me the time of day."

"James and Clara, stay on the line while I pinpoint your location."

"Got it."

Lambert rolled his chair over to Thomas's side of the desk. Together, they entered James's phone into a triangulation program. The system pinged the location after a brief delay.

"I see you," Thomas said into the phone. "You're more like fifteen miles from Wolf Lake. I'll deal with the towing company and get someone to take care of the flat."

"Thank you, Sheriff," the couple said in unison.

"I don't want the two of you to be alone while you wait. It could be an hour or two before I get a tow truck to your location. I'm sending Deputy Lambert. Don't move until he arrives."

"We won't."

The call ended, and Thomas turned to his senior deputy. "You mind driving out there while Emma deals with the press release?"

"Not a problem," Lambert said. "They're a long way from home."

"It's easy to get lost in the countryside."

"I've done it myself."

"As have I," said Thomas. "Get a hold of me on the radio as soon as you reach the Hartleys."

Lambert bounced out of his seat, retrieved his hat, and hurried out the door.

Thomas turned his attention back to the prison database. Aguilar had sent him another hundred names. They were over three hundred now. Too many. He was no closer to finding Hannah's kidnapper.

While he sifted through the suspects, he crossed names off the list whenever he found someone who hadn't been active in the late 1990s through the mid-2000s.

When Lambert's voice came through the radio, Thomas jumped in surprise. The deputy had already arrived.

"The Hartleys are safe, and the tow truck should arrive in a few minutes," Lambert said.

"No damage to their car?"

"Just the blown tire. But they're pretty shook."

"Losing control of your vehicle will do that to you."

"Sure it will, but that's not why they're scared. The Hartleys swear someone was following them."

11

Deputy Lambert flipped the page on his notepad and took more information from James and Clara Hartley.

The husband was of medium height and had an athletic build, reflecting a lifestyle that balanced physical activity with a career that demanded mental acuity. His hair was a dark chestnut, styled in a manner that was both practical and fashionable. His eyes, a deep brown, were intense and alert, as if the blown tire had just occurred. Despite being in his mid-thirties and relatively young, he had an air of confidence; he was a man accustomed to taking charge and making decisions.

Clara stood shorter than James. Her graceful, agile body hinted at a passion for dance or yoga. Her auburn hair hung loose. Like her husband, she looked as if she'd just seen a ghost.

"Tell me again about when you abandoned your car beside the road," Lambert said.

"I couldn't get a cell signal," James said, "and neither could Clara. The wind was blowing toward Wolf Lake, so I figured we'd have trouble getting a connection."

"So you tried to find a signal?"

Clara nodded. "I marched up and down the road, but all I got was a partial bar. None of my calls connected. That's when James got the idea about climbing the hill."

The deputy's hat shielded his eyes from the sun, which was falling through the western sky. Two hours until sunset.

"That's a tough hike. I don't suppose there is a trail."

"A footpath," James said.

That didn't seem right. Why would there be a footpath this far from Treman Mills and Wolf Lake? Nobody owned this land, and hunting season didn't last long enough for a parade of boots to carve a new trail.

"Then what happened?"

"We started up the hill," Clara said. "There was a clearing at the top, but we still couldn't connect."

"And Clara thought she heard footsteps in the forest," James said. He drew himself up, as if feigning bravery.

The wife whirled on him. "Don't start, James. You heard the footsteps too."

"I heard *something*. It could have been animals crawling through the brush."

"Then how do you explain the gun cocking?"

Lambert swung his head toward Clara. "What gun? You never talked about a gun."

James shook his head. "We both heard a clicking sound. It might have been someone cocking a gun. But now that I think about it, maybe it was just a branch snapping."

Clara didn't appear convinced.

"Did you see this person?" Lambert asked, scanning the forest. Pitch-black stretched beyond the first line of trees.

"Nope. We ran, as you might imagine. After we hid for a while, I trekked up the hill again to make sure no one was following us. As far as I could tell, we were alone in the forest."

After breaking down or blowing a tire far from civilization, people often let their imaginations run wild. Lambert wondered if Clara and James were mistaken. Still, he couldn't leave the scene without checking around.

"And there was a graveyard in the clearing," Clara said.

The deputy set one hand on his hip. "A graveyard?"

"Crosses formed with sticks and twine," James said. "There's no reason to believe it's really a cemetery."

Lambert knew a lot about this region. Though he'd grown up in the Midwest, he'd worked in Nightshade County long enough to know its history. Had there been a cemetery here long ago? If so, he didn't recall. The closest town was Treman Mills, and that was ten or fifteen miles from this location. He saw no reason for a graveyard to exist this far from the population bases.

"It was a cemetery," Clara insisted.

The rumbling tow truck's engine broke up the argument before it escalated. Clara smiled for the first time since Lambert had arrived. Not that she seemed like a disagreeable person. Obviously, being stranded had upset her. Lambert might have felt the same had this happened to him.

"Howdy, folks," the bearded tow truck driver said. His name tag read Herbert.

"Glad you found the place," Lambert said.

Herbert tugged on his beard. "Y'all were really out here. That's the way it is with vehicles. Nothing ever goes wrong in the city. Only when you are miles from help."

"Can you get these folks back on the road?"

"Shouldn't take long."

The driver removed tools from his truck and returned to the shoulder, where he kneeled beside the blown tire. He grunted as he fitted the wrench onto the first lug nut. His confidence waned as he applied pressure. The nut refused to budge. He adjusted his grip and exerted greater force. Nothing moved.

"Well, that's odd," Herbert said, trying another. The same result met his efforts. Immovable, as if fused to the bolt.

"I told you the last two nuts were pretty stuck," James said.

Herbert sat back on his heels and wiped his brow with the back of his hand. "I've seen rusted nuts. But these seem like they're welded on. Never in my twenty years . . ." His voice trailed off as he inspected another lug nut.

"Can't you just cut them off?" asked Clara.

The man shook his head. "Not out here, ma'am. I'd need a torch for that, and it's not exactly standard issue in my line of work. Plus, the heat could damage your wheel." He stood, looking at the couple. "I'm sorry, but this looks like a job for the garage. I'll have to tow you in."

James exchanged a glance with Clara, a mixture of frustration and resignation passing between them.

"Do what you have to. We just want to get out of here," James said.

While the tow truck driver worked, Lambert paced the shoulder with one eye on the forested hill. His hand never strayed far from his holster. A graveyard this far from town? And someone cocking a gun? He hoped Clara's imagination had gotten the best of her.

Herbert hooked their car to the tow truck. "All done. Hop in the back, folks, and I'll drive you to the shop."

James didn't seem happy that the car would have to be towed.

Lambert shook Herbert's hand. "Thanks again."

"That's what we're here for. I'll get the crew to fix that bolt. Shouldn't take long."

After the tow truck dragged the Hartley's car away, Lambert stood on the shoulder, wondering about what Clara had said. The hill was steps away. Every time he stared into the trees, a shiver rolled through his body.

He pressed the call button on his radio. "Thomas, Lambert here. You have your ears on?"

The wind tugged at his jacket and made him wish he'd worn something warmer. Now that the sun had perched just above the trees, the temperature was falling.

"Thomas here."

"The Hartleys are on their way back to Treman Mills."

"Is the tire fixed?"

"Couldn't fix it here. Two bolts rusted on."

"Talk about bad luck," Thomas said. "The Hartleys were okay, otherwise?"

"No worse for wear, but the wife still swears someone was following them. She mentioned hearing a gun cock."

"Do you believe her?"

"I'm not sure what to believe, Thomas. The husband wasn't so sure, but he seemed more disturbed than he was willing to admit. My feeling is the situation got the best of them, but I don't want to leave the area until I'm positive it's safe."

"Wait for backup."

"No need. I don't see anyone in sight, and I haven't heard so much as a peep from the forest."

"Regardless, I'm sending two juniors your way."

"You sure that's necessary?" Lambert asked.

"I'd rather be safe than sorry."

Thomas ended the call with a warning to stand down until backup arrived. Lambert intended to follow the sheriff's advice.

Except the tree-covered forest kept giving him the creeps. If there was a makeshift cemetery in the woods, he needed to alert someone. The darn thing should be on a map.

His radio crackled again, but it wasn't Thomas this time. Dispatch was contacting another deputy in the field.

What was the harm in walking to the forest's edge and checking things out? He was certain nobody was hiding inside.

He hopped over the ditch and trudged through brown and gangling knee-high grass. The trees looked down at him. Suddenly, he felt microscopic in their presence.

Lambert placed a hand on an elm. Damn, it was dark past the tree line. He strained to listen over the gusting wind, but no sounds came from the forest.

Until he heard the disturbing laughter.

12

Lambert drew his gun.

Branches rained around him as the wind shook the trees as if they were unruly children in need of correction. Everywhere he looked was dark. So different from the world outside of the forest, where a hazy sun still shone through thin clouds.

Footprints ran to his left and right. They could belong to the Hartleys. Or whoever was chasing them through the woods.

He refused to jump to conclusions. Their stories had differed, and it was anybody's guess who was right. But the prospect of an insane person hiding in the shadows with a gun kept the deputy on edge.

"Thomas, come in."

No response on the radio. Communications had worked fine while he stood along the road, but now nothing functioned. His phone displayed no signal, and his boots struggled on the sloppy terrain. The land would dry out as spring progressed, but he wondered if conditions ever improved this deep in the woods.

"Sheriff, can you hear me?"

A sound to the right cut him short. He pocketed the radio

and aimed the gun toward the noise. Seconds later, a raccoon scurried past. He laughed at himself and felt thankful Aguilar wasn't here to rib him for losing his cool.

This place gave him the creeps. Not that he was afraid of the dark. Never.

Lambert watched the raccoon vanish into the underbrush before moving on. The steep hill loomed before him, almost daring him to climb higher.

Clara had mentioned something about a clearing full of crosses. Crosses made of sticks and twine, as a child might make.

He scanned the forest floor for more footprints but found none. Another branch snapped behind him. He whirled and aimed the gun at a fallen bough. Nothing else.

"Sheriff's department. Who's out here? You're not supposed to hunt out of season."

The wind crooned, and he swore someone chuckled beneath the dirge. Were the Hartleys' stories affecting him, or was someone in the woods, watching and waiting?

He clasped the top button of his jacket and stopped the chill from wrapping its fingers around his neck. Somewhere behind him, a car motored down the road. He imagined the driver rubbernecking to see why a sheriff's cruiser was parked on the shoulder so far from the closest neighborhood.

His powerful legs and long strides took him higher. The air seemed thinner here, though that idea might be in his head too. He wasn't sure where he was, and he understood how James and Clara had lost their way.

The mud slid out from under him as he fell forward. He caught himself with his hands before his head struck the muck and grime. As he turned to look, he came face to face with a broken branch, its jagged edge inches from his eye. Too close for comfort. People could kill themselves out here.

It took another five minutes until the land leveled out and

the trees gave way to a clearing. Here, the weakening light of day made its last stand. He drank in every drop.

Then his attention fell on the overgrown grass and weeds. Where was this supposed cemetery? Clara and James said they'd discovered the crosses on top of the hill, and this forest was too dense to hold another clearing.

But there was nothing here. No crosses or graves. No vampires rising out of the earth.

So why was he trembling? He told himself it was the chill.

Lambert paced through the clearing, examining the ground as he walked. If there were crosses, he didn't see them.

More footprints caught his eye. He kneeled and studied several indentations. James had walked beside Clara. Lambert knew he was in the right location. So where was the graveyard?

The chuckling sound came again from behind the trees.

"Sheriff's department. You're not in trouble, but you shouldn't be out here. Show yourself."

No one answered.

He waited until the breeze abated and listened again. Nothing this time.

Lambert wanted to write off the laughter as nature sounds, but he couldn't. There was another pair of tracks on the ground. He removed his phone and took a picture. The treads told him this person was wearing hiking boots, and they were larger than James's shoes. Yes, a third person had been here.

Standing, he studied the path of tracks before they disappeared into the trees. It sure seemed like the third set was following the first two.

He tried his radio again. "Thomas, it's Lambert. Do you read?"

"Lambert, where are you?"

"Checking out the clearing the Hartleys told me about."

"You should have stood down. A cruiser will arrive soon.

ETA is five minutes. I don't want to ask, but did you find anything to corroborate the Hartleys' stories?"

"No graveyard, no crosses. I'm unsure what they saw. But there are footprints here, Thomas. Three pairs."

A pause. "That's why I told you to wait for backup."

"I didn't think anyone was here. There are no vehicles in the vicinity, and these are the only tracks I've come across."

"The husband and wife mentioned this person carrying a gun," Thomas said. "And you're standing in the open."

Lambert realized what Thomas meant. Anyone could pick him off before he reacted. If a man with a weapon lurked in the forest, Lambert would never see him. One shot was all it would take, and he wasn't wearing Kevlar.

"Point taken. What do you want me to do?"

"Get out of the clearing, but don't leave the forest. No sense climbing up and down that hill and risking your neck. Wait for backup."

"10-4."

He put away the radio and checked his gun. Loaded and ready. Here and there, he noticed tiny black holes in the ground, just wide enough for him to dig his finger into them. What did that mean?

The lengthening shadows played tricks on his eyes. He was seeing ghosts. Not to mention he was a sitting duck.

Lambert abandoned the clearing and entered the trees. He couldn't see his hand in front of his face, the gloom was so thick. Putting one booted foot forward, he noticed how quickly the terrain dropped away. If he slipped, he wouldn't stop tumbling until he shattered his body against a tree.

If someone were hiding in the woods, Lambert couldn't find him. It was probably just a hunter or a hiker. And if this person had wanted to shoot Lambert, he could have done so at any time. James had said he doubted the other man had a gun. There was no reason to believe this person was dangerous.

With nothing to do but wait for backup to arrive, Lambert leaned against a tree.

HIS HANDS CURLED into fists and wrapped around two knife hilts. The gun stuck out of his pocket, but he didn't need it. With the element of surprise on his side, he could take out anyone. Even an armed sheriff's deputy.

The deputy had come so close to ruining everything.

But the killer was a fast thinker. He didn't make mistakes. As soon as he'd seen the deputy enter the forest, he removed the crosses and placed them out of sight.

That damn husband and wife had seen the crosses and told the officer. He should have killed them to keep them from talking. Now he had a problem. Murder the deputy and bring this story to its conclusion? Or stay hidden and hope the officer moved on?

He preferred the knives. They were silent killers. Though he appreciated his gun, people would hear the blast for miles. Even out here, a place he'd chosen because of its isolation, he couldn't guarantee nobody would report the shooting.

Plus, the sheriff's department knew where their deputy was.

What if he tore the knife across the deputy's throat? He would have to move the body so the other officers never found it. Easier said than done. The deputy stood over six feet tall and possessed a powerful physique. He wasn't someone you could toss over your shoulder and carry for a few miles.

Unless he dragged the deputy. Yes, that would work. He could place the body on two fir tree branches.

The killer stepped out from behind the tree. Time to kill the deputy and ensure no one discovered his secrets.

He was nothing more than a shadow in the dark. Undetectable. A predator of the highest order.

The madman crept up on the deputy from behind. He made sure he stepped on the soft bed of pine needles that wouldn't give him away. A few more paces, and the deputy was his.

The whoop of a siren pulled him up short. In an instant, the deputy spun around.

With his breath flying in and out of his lungs, the killer stood with his back against a tree. More officers had arrived. Had the deputy seen him?

When the officer started down the hill, the killer slipped into the darkness.

13

Chelsey blinked. “I’m not sure I understand how this software operates.”

Scout was demonstrating her applications while LeVar sat beside her, offering his own two cents. Raven reclined in a chair and rested her feet on the edge of a desk. Her co-owner seemed amused.

“Don’t act like you understand everything she’s saying,” Chelsey said.

Raven flicked the braids off her shoulder. “I don’t, but it’s funny watching you swim upstream.”

LeVar thumbed through a bookshelf filled with volumes about criminal psychology, cyber security, and investigative techniques as he observed the exchange between the team members.

Scout, energized by the previous night's groundwork, acted like she couldn’t wait to bring Chelsey and Raven up to speed on the technological advancements they were employing to narrow down the stalker's location. Her laptop, now connected to the firm's secure network, displayed an array of open applications and windows.

"Here’s what I have," Scout said. "We're using a combination of natural language processing, or NLP, and machine learning to analyze the writing style of our stalker. This approach helps us identify unique linguistic fingerprints in his messages."

"I thought NLP stood for neuro-linguistic programming," Raven said.

"It does, but in the technology community, NLP means natural language processing."

"One programs a computer, and the other programs a mind."

"Good point. I hadn't thought of that."

Chelsey waved her hands. "Never mind with the acronyms. How accurate is this analysis? Can it differentiate one person's writing from another's? There must be millions of relevant posts."

"It's surprisingly effective. We feed the system samples of the stalker's known communications. The software analyzes everything from word choice to sentence structure and even the rhythm of the writing. Then it compares this profile against posts from various forums and blogs."

"This could be a game-changer in identifying patterns and predicting future behavior," Raven said. "Want to take WLC to the next level? This is how we get there."

"I'm supplementing with heuristic analysis. I set up rules based on the stalker's known behaviors and preferences. Any post that hits these markers gets flagged for further review."

LeVar joined the group at the table. "Scout ran these tools all night. I already have a list of potential matches, but we'll need to refine the search to get more specific."

Now Chelsey understood how the software operated. "This could help find Elliot Saunders' stalker and build a behavioral profile that could be crucial for the prosecution."

Always focused on the human element, Raven added, "This could provide insights into his motives and help us prevent him from harassing anyone else."

"There's more." Scout tapped a manicured nail against the laptop screen. "I'm tracking the IP addresses associated with these flagged posts. We're looking for patterns of movement or frequent locations that might help us pinpoint his physical whereabouts."

Chelsey absorbed the information. They had brand-new tools to stop this digital stalker before he escalated. And he *would* escalate, given enough time. "What do we need to do next?"

"As we refine our search and gather more data, we can cross-reference the locations with Saunders' known movements and any public events he attended."

Scout clicked through several windows on her laptop to show the progress they had made. There had to be a few hundred names worth investigating.

They had made this much progress in one night? It baffled Chelsey that the software had worked while they slept. Talk about efficiency.

"All right, team. Scout and LeVar, I want you to filter these names to a few dozen likely candidates and send them to Raven's email."

"On it, boss woman," LeVar said.

"And LeVar, if you complete this task by eleven o'clock, I'll spring for two dozen donuts from The Broken Yolk."

"For *realz*?"

"Motivated?"

"Hundred percent."

While the others worked, Chelsey took her place at her desk. As the founder of Wolf Lake Consulting, she could have built a private office down the hall, but that didn't fit her vision. This was a team, and she was a member like everyone else. Plus, these were her friends, and they were closer than any family she had.

She paid two bills and pulled up the latest financial statements. A grin dimpled her cheeks. If it weren't for Raven, the firm would have gone under. She was so thankful for her best friend. Making Raven co-owner of Wolf Lake Consulting had been her smartest move. Though Raven was a badass investigator with a nose for ferreting criminals out of hiding, she was a business whiz.

Then there was LeVar, the reformed Harmon gangster who worked as one of Thomas's junior deputies. The twenty-year-old studied criminal justice at the community college and would soon transfer to Kane Grove University, which housed the premier law enforcement program in the region. LeVar could take over this business and make it flourish.

And who could forget Scout? Was this girl really only sixteen? The teen brought more to the table than some of the most experienced investigators Chelsey had encountered. Her technological skills complemented the team in ways no one else could.

Wolf Lake Consulting was the number one private investigation firm in Nightshade County for a reason. Each of them gave unique contributions.

After LeVar and Scout sent the first list of names to Raven, Chelsey called everyone together.

"LeVar, you're our profiling expert. Based on the messages sent to Elliot Saunders, what can you tell us about our suspect?"

LeVar crossed his legs at the ankles and placed his hands behind his head. "You want my opinion?"

"I need your expertise."

"Are donuts involved?"

"Yes, LeVar, yes. Donuts are involved."

The off-duty deputy unfolded his legs and leaned forward. He leaped into his role as their in-house profiler. "All right, check it. Based on the venom in these messages, our stalker dude's primary fuel seems to be jealousy, straight up. He's not just some random troll looking for a laugh. This guy's got a vendetta."

"Jealousy? That's his motive?"

"Yeah, for real. And the way he crafts those messages, all meticulous and coded? He's definitely got some tech chops. Probably works in high tech himself, or did until he got axed. That could've sparked the whole jealousy trip."

Raven chimed in. "So you're saying this is personal for him? Saunders represents what he lost or never achieved?"

"All in. And peep this—the escalation in his messages? That's textbook for someone spiraling. Our stalker's on the edge. Feels like he's got nothing to lose. That makes him dangerous."

Scout adjusted her glasses. "If he's that skilled, he's probably covering his tracks online. That's why the IP tracking is so hard."

"Word. But the dude's human. He's gonna slip, and when he does . . ."

Chelsey smiled at LeVar's insight. "How do we provoke that slip?"

LeVar's own grin turned sly. "We keep pushing his buttons. Make him think Saunders is winning, thriving even more than ever. Our stalker's ego won't be able to handle it."

"That's risky," Raven said. "It could provoke him into doing something drastic."

"But it could also rush him into making a mistake," said Chelsey. "Okay, team. Let's refine our list, monitor Saunders' digital footprint, and prepare our next moves. LeVar, your insights have given us a solid profile to work with. Scout, keep digging into those forums and blogs, but keep the profile in mind. Raven, work on a plan to escalate our target without putting Saunders in danger."

"What about me?" LeVar asked.

"Choose your donut flavors. You earned them."

LeVar's laughter filled the room. "Bet. Make sure there's some jelly in there."

As Chelsey gathered her keys, Thomas phoned her.

"How's your day, hon?" he asked.

She donned a jacket with the phone clamped between her shoulder and ear. "Doing great. How about you?"

"Not bad. We're still working on this kidnapping cold case."

"I wish we had the resources to help you."

"Don't apologize. The county funds the department well. Have you made any progress on the Elliot Saunders investigation?"

Chelsey stepped outside. With the lunch hour approaching, the streets were getting crowded. "Scout just showed us an amazing way to track people on the internet. I'll have her teach you sometime this week."

"Catch the bad guy yet?"

"We will," she said. "Especially now that we have a profile to work with."

"Did LeVar come up with the profile?"

"Indeed. His classes are paying off."

"Hey, Chelsey. I wanted to give you a heads up that I need to work late this evening. Don't expect me for supper."

She exhaled. "Same here. What about Tigger and Jack?"

"Naomi said she'd feed them and take out Jack."

"Thank goodness for friendly neighbors." A horn honked as she stepped off the curb. "I'd better end this call before I play Frogger in the middle of Wolf Lake. People drive like maniacs."

They said their goodbyes as Chelsey jogged down the sidewalk to The Broken Yolk. Maybe by the time she returned, the team would have caught their target.

14

Between Emma's skills at writing press releases and Thomas's contacts, all of Nightshade County knew Hannah's case was open again. Now they just needed a member of the public to remember an event, a face, or a vehicle and step forward.

The journalist appeared drained from the process. Not from the work, but from remembering her lost friend. He couldn't imagine how difficult the years had been. Had she sought therapy? She blamed herself for not walking to the store with Hannah, but what might have happened had she done so? It wasn't beyond the realm of possibility that the killer would have taken both girls.

And that's how he thought of the kidnapper—a killer. The girls had never been found. He was a serial killer of children.

Yet Thomas didn't voice his opinion in front of Emma. She had enough on her mind without imagining her friend's body tossed into a ditch and left for the animals.

Thomas would catch this man if he were free. If the killer were serving time, he'd ensure the psychopath never again saw the light of day.

He was so engrossed in his thoughts that he didn't see Emma slide into the chair across from his desk. He pulled his eyes away from the computer screen.

"The press release looks excellent," he said. "I have a good feeling we'll get some bites."

"Let's hope."

"How are you handling all of this? It must be a lot."

"It is," she said, idly tracing a circle on his desk with her finger. "But I'll do anything for Hannah and the other girls. Can I see the list of incarcerated men who fit the profile?"

He slid three sheets of printed names across the desk.

She leafed through the names and looked up. "This many?"

"Afraid so. We have our work cut out for us."

Down the hall, Lambert removed his hat and plopped onto his chair. Mud stained his pants as if he'd rolled down the forest hill.

"I should speak to my deputy," Thomas said. "You're welcome to stay in my office and gather your thoughts. Feel free to close the door if you want privacy."

"Thanks, but I need to clear my head. I think I'll take a walk."

"That's fine. We'll be here when you're ready to dive into the investigation again."

He watched her go, unsure why he felt a prickle of unease when she stepped outside. Gloaming had spread across the sky, and many village businesses had closed for the day.

"Nobody in the forest?" Thomas asked, standing beside Lambert's desk.

"Not a soul. But I swear . . ."

A vein pulsed on the side of Lambert's head.

"What were you about to say?"

"I swore someone was watching us."

"Well, you found a third set of footprints, and the Hartleys claimed someone was in the woods," Thomas said.

"Clara made that claim; James, not so much. I'm relatively certain someone else was there, but it could have been a hunter, a hiker. Who knows?"

"I'll have a deputy cruise past the forest entrance once or twice a day."

"Thomas, anyone could hide up there with no one noticing. You can't believe how thick those woods are."

"But if this hunter parks along the road, we'll know someone is there."

"Yeah, that's true," said Lambert. "Anyhow, I'm happy the Hartleys made it back to town. James just messaged me. The garage removed the lug nuts, changed the tire, and got them on the road."

"All's well that ends well. Hey, you skipped dinner."

"Not hungry."

"I can't have my deputies missing meals. Run out and grab food." Thomas removed money from his wallet. "And get me a sandwich too. My stomach is growling."

"You don't have to pay, boss man."

"Yes, I do. When you become the sheriff, you can flip for the bill."

Lambert laughed. "No offense, Thomas, but I don't want your job. Too much pressure and bureaucracy."

"But it pays well."

The deputy raised a quizzical eyebrow. "It does?"

"Okay, maybe not. But I have Shepherd Systems to fall back on."

Lambert accepted the money.

As Thomas took a breather, he glanced out the window. Full dark was approaching, and Emma hadn't returned.

He rose to check the sidewalk just as the journalist entered the building. Why had her departure unnerved him so much?

"What did I miss?" she asked, setting a brown paper bag on his desk.

"Not much." He took a whiff. "Is that what I think it is?"

"Coffee and croissants from The Broken Yolk. Ever heard of it?" She shook her head. "Of course you have. You work five blocks from the cafe."

"I'm quite familiar with The Broken Yolk."

"I figured it would be a long evening."

"You didn't have to buy. I sent Lambert to grab dinner. Should I text him and ensure he brings you something?" he asked.

"No, I doubt I could keep down a full meal."

He assessed her from across the desk—sunken eyes, pale skin. "How was your walk?"

"I needed it. You know, Wolf Lake hasn't changed much since I graduated from high school."

"Time moves slower here."

The croissants and coffee gave him a jolt of energy. He wasn't convinced sweets lent healthy energy, but it was better than starving. Lambert returned, and the three of them gathered around the office table and ate while they shared their opinions.

"I'm seeing more and more incidences of abducted children across the border into Pennsylvania," Lambert said.

"Still within a hundred-mile radius?" Thomas asked.

"Yeah, but that's grounds for bringing in the FBI. Are you considering the option?"

"I might give Agents Gardy and Bell at the Behavioral Analysis Unit a call."

Neil Gardy and Scarlett Bell had helped Thomas with multiple cases. He knew they were busy, but they would drop everything if he needed a profile. With a little arm-twisting, the agents might even come to Wolf Lake and help him investigate. But he didn't want to take up too much of their time. They were chasing a man who was probably dead or behind bars. The lack of kidnappings in recent years convinced Thomas the threat had ended.

"Have you spoken with law enforcement in Pennsylvania?" Emma asked.

"Not yet, but I might take a drive tomorrow and hit as many places as I can along the way."

"Over the years, I've looked into similar abductions across New York State, but I never realized this guy crossed state lines. Did you ever look into Nolan Trevino?"

"I spoke with a few of his family members. He's not our guy."

"How sure are you?" Lambert asked, wiping his mouth with the back of his hand.

"Positive. Listen, I knew Trevino for years. Yes, he spent time alone in the park while children were playing. He didn't understand that doing so made people nervous. I'm telling you, the guy who abducted Hannah and the other girls was someone else. I'll prove it."

Lambert met eyes with Emma across the table.

"Sheriff?"

Thomas jumped. He hadn't realized a junior deputy was standing behind him. Lambert chuckled.

"Yes, deputy?"

"A call came in. Neighbors reported a suspicious vehicle outside a park on the other side of the village."

Emma sat up. "Near the elementary school?"

"Correct."

"Thank you," Thomas said. "I'll look into it."

As the other deputy returned to his work, Emma donned her coat. "That's the park Hannah and I walked past every day."

Coincidence? For the last few hours, the media had asked for information about the old kidnappings. People were on high alert and might overreact to a strange vehicle.

Still, an unrecognized person outside a park where children played was worth investigating.

"I can't allow you to come with me," Thomas said to Emma.

"Why not?"

"Because it might be dangerous, and you're not a trained officer."

"What if I recognize the person in the vehicle?"

She had a point, but it wasn't worth the risk. By the time he reached the park, the stranger would probably be gone.

"Head back to your hotel, Emma. We'll work again tomorrow."

Lambert shrugged into his jacket. "All right, boss man. Let's catch a predator."

15

"I'm afraid this media blitz is backfiring," Lambert said.

Thomas couldn't argue with his deputy. Sitting behind the wheel in their cruiser, he rubbed his eyes. Why had the neighbors reported a Village Parks Department vehicle as suspicious? People were seeing phantoms, and that was exactly what he didn't want. They'd issued the press release to jog memories, not to make everyone paranoid.

"We can't keep responding to false alarms," said Thomas.

"What do you think we should do?"

"There's no turning back time. The information is out there, and we have to hope it does some good. In the meantime, I feel like we should make sure the kids in Wolf Lake are safe."

"What do you have in mind?"

"A meeting of some sort. Pull everyone together and discuss what happened in the past, teach best practices that kids and their parents should follow."

"Hopefully, get everyone to stop panicking." Lambert adjusted himself in the passenger's seat. "What now?"

"We'll head back to the station and call it a day. I'll brief Emma about what happened tomorrow."

"Thomas, what do you make of her?"

"Why do you ask?"

"She went through hell and might not have her head on straight. How many years has she researched these abductions? Work on a case that long, and you lose perspective."

"I can't put myself in her shoes," said Thomas. "It's true that she's been through a lot. But I trust her judgment. So far, she's provided solid information and ideas."

But Thomas understood Lambert's point. Had it not been for Emma, they wouldn't be sitting here in the dark after responding to a false alarm. This would only get worse as people spotted more strangers. Pretty soon, anyone visiting Wolf Lake would come under suspicion.

Thomas drove them back to the office, where they gathered their belongings and checked out for the night. He was excited to see Chelsey and the pets again. On his way home, a full moon rose over the lake. The haunted reflection stretched across the water and rippled in the waves.

Summer wasn't far away. Soon, kids of all ages would ride bikes and play outdoors without supervision.

He needed to protect the children of Wolf Lake.

THE GIRL HAD auburn hair hanging to her shoulders. At twelve years of age, Tiffany Harris was aware of what had happened to that Hannah Clarke girl a long time ago. Her parents had seen it on the news last night, and all day the teachers at school had discussed strangers and safety. Rumor had it they would attend an assembly tomorrow. A sheriff's deputy might even speak.

Today was warmer than yesterday, but it wasn't mild enough for her to remove her jacket. She sat on a bench in Greenwood Park, which sprawled across eighteen acres between the elementary and middle schools. On a typical day, she would open a thriller book—one of those Lisa Gardner novels her parents didn't think she was old enough to read—and spend an hour engrossed in a mystery. Not this time. Jake Thompson was here, and he was a year older and altogether perfect. Her cheeks heated whenever he was near.

"I don't get what they're so excited about," Jake said, referring to the teachers' warnings. "That girl disappeared in the 1990s. Do you realize how long ago that was? Did they even have electricity back then?"

"They just want us to take things seriously."

"Take *what* seriously? The kidnapper hasn't come around since then. It was probably a family member who took Hannah."

"How do you know that?"

"'Cause my dad told me it's usually someone who knows the kid, not a stranger."

That was true. She'd heard the same on a television show.

Jake tossed a baseball into the air and caught it with a gloved hand. He wore a cap backwards, and though it wasn't warm enough, the boy showed off his legs in athletic shorts. She'd watched him play last summer. He was good. That day, he'd hit a triple and never noticed how loudly she was cheering from the stands. Until recently, he hadn't known she existed.

Mom had warned her about Jake. He was a troublemaker, a rebel according to her parents. Not that Mom or Dad should talk. They both listened to some band called The Foo Fighters.

Now Jake threw the ball against a wooden fort erected beside a swing set and caught the rebound. Each time the baseball struck the side, it sounded like a gunshot and made her wince.

"Maybe you shouldn't do that," she said.

"Why not?"

"Because little kids play here."

"They're not here now. We're alone."

With that, he winked. She blushed.

"It's not polite to—"

She stopped when a shadow moved among the trees across the way. Aiming her phone, she snapped a picture.

"What's wrong?"

"Jake, there's someone over there."

"Where? I don't see anyone."

Tiffany pointed.

After studying the trees for a moment, he shrugged. "There's no one watching us."

"But I saw him."

"Oh, really? What did he look like?"

"Like . . . a shadow."

He snickered. "That's descriptive. You're letting all those stories get to you."

"No," she said. "He was there. I swear."

"All right. If you're convinced, let's walk to the trees and check things out."

"That's a bad idea."

"What are you afraid of? If some creeper is hanging out, I'll put a fastball between his eyes."

Hesitantly, she rose from the bench and fixed her backpack over one shoulder. "If it really is a stranger, promise you won't run and leave me alone."

"Don't you trust me?"

She did. And when he held her hand, she stopped feeling afraid. Reaching the far side of the park took a few moments, but it seemed like seconds with her heart fluttering. He had that effect on her.

When they approached the trees, he put his hands on his hips. "See? There's no one here, Tiffany."

As if she needed convincing, she pushed the brush aside and peered into the shaded area. He was right.

Tiffany followed Jack back to the swings and the park bench. As they walked, she sensed eyes on her back. But when she turned her head, there was nobody watching.

His voice took on a conspiratorial tone as they sat. He studied the empty playground as if to ensure their solitude. "You know, Tiff, for someone who reads thriller books, you're pretty nervous."

Tiffany rolled her eyes but couldn't suppress the smile tugging at her lips. "I'm not spooked. Just cautious."

"Cautious, huh?" Jake leaned back, stretching his arms across the back of the bench, his casual posture belying the keen interest in his eyes. "Well, if you're into mysteries, you'll love the story of the disappearing shadows of Greenwood Park."

Tiffany turned to face him. "What on earth are you talking about?"

"Legend has it that as dusk falls, the shadows in the park move on their own, detached from their owners. They say these shadows belong to kids who vanished in the park. They're trapped between worlds, looking for someone to take their place."

She didn't believe him, but that didn't stop her hands from trembling.

"That sounds made up."

"Maybe, but my buddy's older brother swore he saw a shadow move right next to him, like it was trying to grab his shoulder. Since then, kids dare each other to stay in the park till dusk, hoping to see the shadows or, you know, prove they're brave enough."

The suggestion hung in the air between them, an unspoken challenge. Tiffany weighed her rational disbelief against the thrill of the unknown. "You really believe that?"

Jake tossed the ball into the air and caught it without looking. "Doesn't matter if I believe it. But wouldn't it be cool to check it out? Unless you're too scared."

She hesitated, torn between her desire to appear brave in Jake's eyes and her caution. The appeal of the adventure, coupled with the chance to spend more time with him, tipped the scales. "Okay, we'll stay. But not until it gets dark. I need to get home for dinner."

"Deal." Jake's smile broadened.

They settled into a comfortable silence, watching the sun track across the sky. She kept checking the time. If she was late for dinner and Mom found out that she'd spent the afternoon with Jake, she would be in trouble.

While they waited for something to happen and for these supposed shadows to come alive, she spotted movement across the park. Someone was behind the trees again. She didn't tell him this time. He'd only laugh and make fun of her.

But she never looked away from the trees.

That was when she noticed he was staring across the park at the same spot.

"You know, maybe this wasn't such a great idea," he said.

"What happened to putting a fastball between a creeper's eyes?"

"Let's get out of here, Tiff."

16

The walk next door to Scout's house was short, but to LeVar it felt like a journey to a new world, one where physics notes were his passport, and Scout's bedroom the uncharted territory.

This wasn't the first time he'd entered her room, but she was sixteen now and no longer resembled the shy, nerdy girl who'd spent her early teenage years in a wheelchair. She'd called and asked him to help her study for a physics exam.

High school physics was three years ago for him, but he remembered an equation or two. Anyone who remembered LeVar from his gang days would never have guessed he'd been a decent student. Perhaps more than decent. Twice he'd flirted with the honor roll before falling a few tenths of a point short. A guidance counselor attempted to put him on the straight and narrow and unleash his untapped potential, but LeVar hadn't been interested.

Everything changed when Sheriff Thomas Shepherd saved his mother's life and gave LeVar a safe place to stay. For free. These days, he paid a pittance to rent the guest house, and always felt he should do more. More than once, he'd considered breaking away and renting a house closer to Wolf Lake Consulting or the sheriff's department, but he couldn't bring himself to do so. He loved Scout and Naomi, Thomas and Chelsey, the pets, and living along the lake. What more could he want out of life?

When he climbed the deck to the sliding glass door that led into the Mournings' kitchen, he almost returned to the guest house. What was he doing? He respected Scout more than anyone he knew, and he couldn't deny the growing attraction he felt for her.

Not that he would ever take advantage of their friendship. He was twenty. She was still in high school.

The insane part was Scout's mother Naomi had no issue with them studying behind closed doors. The woman trusted him. He couldn't let her down.

Naomi noticed him standing there before he worked up the courage to knock. She let him into the kitchen, which was redolent of meatloaf and a savory sauce that made his mouth water.

"Thanks for agreeing to help Scout study for her exam," she said, wiping her hands on a towel.

He adjusted the backpack on his shoulder. "Anytime."

"This is an important test. If she wants Kane Grove University to accept her, she needs to keep her grades up."

"*Aight*, I'll see what I remember."

Naomi kissed his cheek. "Always so humble. I'm sure you remember plenty."

He didn't know how to respond. Everyone placed so much trust in him. Had he earned it?

"You down with Scout graduating early and heading off to college?"

She weighed her words before answering. "I was nervous at the beginning, but Kane Grove is nearby. And it helps that you'll be there."

He swallowed. “I’ll monitor her activities like a PI. Make sure she doesn’t do keg stands at frat parties.”

Naomi covered her mouth and laughed. “You crack me up. Scout is waiting for you in the bedroom.”

“You sure you don’t want me to give you the dibs on Kane Grove University? I know the place inside out.”

“We have time to discuss the specifics. Go on. She’s struggling with equations.”

He wished she would have kept him longer or expressed concern about him working with Scout behind a closed door. Why weren’t they studying at the kitchen table or in the living room?

Light spilled into the hallway from her half-open bedroom door. It wasn’t too late to turn around.

“LeVar, is that you?”

Okay, now it was too late.

“Yo, Scout.”

He pushed the door open. The room was a blend of childhood memories and teenage aspirations, with band posters on the walls and physics books spread across the bed.

Scout sat cross-legged among the textbooks. Her focus shifted to him. "I'm so glad you're here. Physics is killing me."

He snickered as he set down his backpack and extracted his old physics notes. "Let's see what we can do about that. Maybe we should sit at your desk."

She suddenly realized she was on the bed. “Oh, yeah. That would be better.”

Taking a seat on a rolling chair, LeVar opened a notebook to a page filled with equations. He’d scribbled notes in the margins years ago. Scout scooted closer, their arms brushing as they leaned over the notes. The contact sent an unexpected jolt through him, and he shifted to maintain some distance.

"Okay, let's start with the basics. Newton's laws of motion—they're the foundation."

As he explained the principles, using the margin of his notebook to sketch diagrams, Scout nodded along, her brow furrowed in concentration. She wore a plaid miniskirt, white socks, and a blouse. Her sneakers sat in the corner. Every so often, their knees brushed, a simple accident of proximity, but each touch made LeVar's heart race, reminding him of the fine line he was walking.

"You explain the concept a lot better than my teacher," she said. "That makes so much more sense. You're pretty good at this stuff."

He offered a smile, but inside he was wrestling with the growing tension between their friendship and the feelings he was trying so hard to ignore. As much as he tried to repress them, he couldn't.

"Don't sleep on my mad skills."

The words left his mouth, and he wanted to pull them back. Including Scout and sleeping in the same sentence was dangerous territory. He still couldn't believe they'd fallen asleep side by side during the worst blizzard in decades. They'd been alone in his guest house. Anything could have happened.

Nothing happened.

It helped to remind himself.

They moved on to discussing vectors and forces, with Scout growing more confident at each problem they solved. As the evening wore on, the room shrank. Energy charged the air.

At one point, she reached for a textbook and her hand brushed his. The contact lingered for a heartbeat longer than necessary, leaving him struggling to refocus on the task.

"Uh, let's tackle another problem," he said as he turned the page to a new set of equations.

"Yeah, sure."

Her cheeks reddened.

As he searched for an equation to challenge her, he thought back to the conversation with Naomi. Was Scout emotionally mature enough to transition from high school to college?

Of course she was. Who was he kidding? The girl had her life together, certainly more than he did.

He pictured them eating in the cafeterias, studying at the library, and walking to class. Sure, she was sixteen today. But eighteen would arrive before either of them realized. Then what? Would a relationship become fair game?

While they worked, the undercurrent of unspoken feelings added a layer of complexity to their interactions. He cleared his throat, determined to guide her through a challenging equation that dealt with the conservation of energy.

"Check it. Let's dive into something a bit more complex. This one stumped me back in the day."

He pointed at an equation filled with variables and symbols.

"So, the total energy in a closed system remains constant?" she asked.

"You got it. Energy can't be created or destroyed, just transformed. Like when a rollercoaster goes up and down hills. The potential energy converts to kinetic energy and back."

He gave her a problem to solve, and she completed the equation in seconds.

"Is this right?"

"Nailed it."

She squealed and threw her arms around his shoulders. "You're the best friend anyone could ask for, LeVar."

He extricated himself from her grasp. She seemed to realize what she'd done and lowered her head, pretending to engross herself in the physics notes.

"Sorry for overstepping my bounds," she said.

"Nah, it's all good." He searched for a way to change the

subject. "Yo, Chelsey and Raven can't stop talking about those machine language apps you set up. Kinda ironic, isn't it?"

"What's ironic?"

"Using AI to catch some dude stalking an AI developer."

"I suppose you're right." She pushed the hair off her forehead. "That's the work I want to do someday, LeVar. Whether it's for the FBI or a small-town investigations firm, I want to outthink criminals and keep people safe. That's why this exam has me so flustered. If I blow it, there's no chance I'll get into Kane Grove early. Or ever."

"Hey, stop with the defeatist talk. That's not you."

"Yeah, I know. It's just a ton of pressure."

"Only because you see it that way. There's nothing stopping you from pulling back and graduating high school with your classmates."

A hurt look clouded her eyes. "But we'd miss out on attending college together. Don't you want that?"

"Course I do. But I don't want you to push yourself too hard."

She snapped her textbook shut. "And that's why I need to graduate early. I need to prove that I can handle this challenge."

"Nobody expects you to."

"Nobody but me."

17

When the bell rang and school dismissed, Tiffany stuffed her homework into a backpack and hustled toward the exit. Each day grew a little milder, and she'd worn shorts today despite her mother's disapproval.

Laughter and shouts bounced off the hallway walls. Freedom beckoned beyond the two double doors, which led to the outside world. A line of school buses corralled her classmates.

She was hoping to find Jake and come up with an excuse to walk home with him. Her disappointment grew when she spotted him with Nicky, another boy on the middle school baseball team.

"Tiff, over here," Jake called.

Nicky smirked, as if in on a secret joke. She started down the sidewalk to them.

"I was just telling Nicky about the park and how you ran off," he said.

"I remember you running too," she pointed out.

"Come on, Tiff, admit it. You were scared of your own shadow."

Tiffany rolled her eyes, a playful smile dancing on her lips. "Oh, please. You were the one who jumped out of his skin. I've never seen you run that fast."

Nicky chuckled, nudging Jake in the ribs. "Yeah, man, Tiffany's got you there. I've seen you run before. It's like you're training to become an Olympic sprinter."

Their banter continued as the school faded into the distance. Jake tried to save face, and Tiffany was delighted that Nicky was taking her side. The trio reached the edge of their neighborhood, where the streets grew quiet and the houses sparse. On a neglected plot of land, an abandoned house made her stop in her tracks.

Stories surrounded the place. Kids swore this was where the creeper had taken Hannah Clarke. They said he'd killed her upstairs and hidden her body parts in the walls.

The air seemed to chill as they passed the dilapidated fence. Dark windows watched through empty eyes.

Jake turned to her. “No more ghost stories. This place is haunted.”

“There's no chance the kidnapper brought that girl here. The sheriff's department would have found him.”

“Are you sure about that?”

She wasn't, but saying so steadied her nerves. “It's not haunted.”

Jake shared a mischievous grin with Nick. “Then there's nothing to be afraid of. Kind of like pretend shadows in the park. I dare you to go inside. See if it's really haunted or just another boring old house.”

Nicky egged her on. "Yeah, Tiffany. Show us you're not afraid."

Her heart skipped a beat. Entering the old house seemed crazy, but backing down in front of Jake and Nicky was equally unsettling. She hesitated as her mind conjured images of apparitions.

"Come on, it's just an old house. What's the worst that could happen?" Jake asked. "We'll wait outside and make sure nothing happens."

"Promise?"

"Sure."

Tiffany glanced at the house's eerie silhouette, framed against the sky. Broken windows allowed animals to crawl into the downstairs. An unhinged shutter banged against the wall in the wind. A part of her wanted to dismiss the dare, to laugh it off and continue home where safety and normalcy awaited. Yet she wondered what secrets lay hidden in the house. If she survived this dare, no one would ever question her bravery. She would achieve instant celebrity status.

Tiffany squared her shoulders, her decision made. "Fine. But you two are coming with me. If we're going to explore a haunted house, we're doing it together."

Jake and Nicky exchanged glances, the reality of the challenge settling in. What had started as a joke had become a test of courage.

"Yeah," Nicky said. "We're not scared, are we, Jake?"

Jake blanched but followed his friend to the house. As they approached the abandoned home, the playful banter faded.

The gate emitted a rusty squeal, a shriek extending far beyond the confines of the yard. They were crossing a dangerous threshold. The exterior bore the marks of neglect. Paint peeled away in large strips, and the wooden siding warped and rotted. The windows, shattered and grimy, offered a glimpse into the darkness within.

She prayed the front door would be locked. But of course it wasn't.

As Jake opened the door, it groaned on its hinges, a sound so filled with despair it seemed to emanate from the soul of the house. A wave of musty air rushed out to greet them, making her nose wrinkle in disgust.

Stepping inside, she found herself in a space that time had forgotten. A broken picture frame lay discarded on the floor. The faces of its subjects had faded away to nothing. Nearby, a child's toy—a teddy bear—lay covered in dust with one remaining eye. Dusty furniture, draped in decaying fabrics, offered a glimpse into the lives that once filled these rooms.

"Nothing downstairs," Jake said.

Tiffany lifted her chin. "See? I told you it wasn't haunted. You were just trying to scare me again. It didn't work."

"Then let's go up," said Nicky.

The staircase led into the unknown. She wanted to turn and run, but then they would laugh. Instead, she led the way up the steps. Jake and Nicky's bravado had waned, their laughter now replaced by anxious glances.

At the top, she came upon a long hallway. Doors lined the corridor on either side, each one slightly ajar, as if tempting them to enter. The air here was cooler. She could feel Jake and Nicky's presence beside her, though she dared not turn her head to look. If she did, something terrible would rush out of the shadows.

Then it occurred to her: What if a person hadn't kidnapped Hannah Clarke? What if the poor girl had strolled home, just like Tiffany, and dared herself to enter the abandoned house? And what if some unspeakable creature had leaped out from behind one of these doors and torn the girl apart with knife-edged claws?

"First door," Jake said. "Let's try it."

She couldn't place the smell inside—until she recognized the remnants of a fast-food meal. The wrapper lay discarded near a makeshift bed in the corner, where a worn pillow hinted at someone's presence. Tiffany's stomach churned. This wasn't a lighthearted adventure but a real-life horror story.

She realized that the upstairs windows lent views of the sidewalk, where anyone could watch kids strolling past after school.

"Someone is here," she whispered.

"Someone *was* here," Nicky said.

"No. He's inside the house. Can't you feel it?"

Each of them recognized what she meant. They were not alone.

The sense of being watched, which Tiffany tried to dismiss, clung to her.

Out of the silent dread, a sound pierced the stillness—a thump from the end of the hallway.

"Is that the house settling?" Jake asked.

She stepped deeper into the room. "I don't think so."

"We have to get out of here."

"But if someone is waiting in the hallway . . ."

Jake stood in front of her and raised his voice. "Whoever is here, I'm calling the sheriff. You'd better get out of here before he shows up."

Nicky stared at his friend as though the boy had lost his mind. Now the unknown presence knew where to find them.

She listened at the door. Jake started to talk until she pressed a finger against her lips.

For what seemed like an eternity, she waited and listened. Silence followed. They needed to make a run for the door. It was now or never.

She didn't need to voice her opinion. The two boys understood.

Without a word, they burst out of the room and raced down the hallway. She descended the stairs in a blur, not daring to look back, not stopping until she reached the front door and leaped off the porch.

Nobody slowed until they were two blocks away. There, they collapsed on a lawn, panting.

"We have to tell someone," Jake said.

Nicky didn't appear convinced. "My parents will kill me."

"The sheriff needs to know," Tiffany said, lifting her phone. "If you won't call, I will."

Jake looked at Nicky, who shrugged his shoulders.

As no argument came, she dialed.

18

Thomas set down the phone.

Interesting. Rosetta Harris, who lived a few blocks from the middle school with her husband and daughter, claimed Tiffany and two friends had entered an abandoned house near the school and discovered evidence that someone had been inside.

Squatters? That was a possibility.

He knew the house well. Someone with a wrecking ball should have destroyed the structure years ago. Every Halloween, the abandoned property attracted kids on dares. Last October, he'd devoted two deputies to canvas the neighborhood. He wished he could order the home's demolition.

What about Tiffany's assertion that someone had chased them out of the house? Again, it could have been a squatter, though Wolf Lake saw little of that. Someone spying on kids on their way home troubled him more. Had Hannah Clarke's kidnapper watched the girl from inside the house then snatched her when nobody was paying attention?

Now someone was hanging out inside the abandoned home again.

"Boss man," Lambert said, knocking on the office door to get Thomas's attention. "I couldn't get Agents Bell and Gardy on the line, but the Behavioral Analysis Unit will provide us with the kidnapper's profile. All I have to do is send them the cases we've uncovered so far."

"Do it. We'll take all the help we can get."

Outside the window, shoppers hurried from store to store. With dinnertime in the rearview mirror, village businesses were closing their doors.

A stack of convicted criminals towered on the edge of his desk. Too many to vet on his own.

What Thomas needed was someone to share the workload. Wolf Lake Consulting was busy with the Elliot Saunders investigation, but maybe Chelsey and Raven could lend a hand.

He dialed LeVar's number.

~

THE INTERIOR of The Broken Yolk cafe made his mouth water.

At a table in the back of the establishment, LeVar sat across from Chelsey and Scout. He'd made it a point to seat himself kitty-corner to the teenager. Yesterday's study session made him worry their relationship was heading in the wrong direction.

Again.

Hadn't they established boundaries and agreed to be *just friends* a month ago? The potential for a relationship kept returning. He felt like he was playing tennis, volleying his desires across the court so they no longer tempted him.

Raven returned with the food and set it in the center of the table. The Broken Yolk, where LeVar worked a few hours a week, had begun making dinner items after Christmas. He knew from experience that they were among the finest eateries in the village.

"Everything here is amazing," he said before Raven passed the paper bags to the others. "I can tell what the meal is without looking."

"Really?" Raven asked. "I have my doubts."

"Don't think so? I'll recognize each item with my eyes closed."

"You'll cheat."

"What we need is a blindfold," Chelsey said.

"Kinky," he said. Scout laughed, and he wished he hadn't chosen that word. "I don't have a blindfold. Give me your baseball cap."

Raven removed her cap and handed it over. "Pull it over your eyes. I don't want you to sneak a peek."

"Would I cheat you, sis?"

"You might."

He did as she asked. "Pass me the first dish. I'll tell you what it is."

Across the table, a bag opened. The scents hit his nose. "The richness of this sauce," he gestured with a fork towards the meal, "is all about the slow-cooked tomatoes. And this crust on the chicken parm with spaghetti? You'll taste a blend of panko and Parmesan. A classic."

Scout said, "Okay, Mr. Chef. How about we put that palate to a more grueling test?"

Raven organized the challenge, arranging samples from their order on a separate plate. "All right, LeVar, no peeking."

Chelsey, trying to stifle her giggles, slid the first sample towards him. "Let's start easy," she said as LeVar leaned forward, his nose twitching as he sniffed the offering.

With each taste, his expressions ranged from concentrated to utterly baffled, his guesses punctuated by the team's laughter. "Is that the veggie lasagna?" he ventured at one point, only to hear Scout's delighted laugh when he was completely off the mark.

Raven and Chelsey provided a running commentary.

"And here we see, ladies and gentlemen, a rare miss by the great eater himself," Chelsey announced as LeVar mistook chicken for eggplant.

LeVar played up his reactions for laughs, guessing with exaggerated confidence or dismay at his errors. He correctly identified more dishes than not. After he finished, he stood and bowed to their applause.

"Thank you, thank you. I'll be here all week," he said, removing the blindfold.

Raven, holding an invisible microphone, summed up the event. "Clearly, LeVar's expertise comes from his round-the-clock practice. Eating is his passion, and he's dedicated to his craft 24/7."

The table erupted into laughter again, with Chelsey adding, "Just wait. In a few years, we'll need to widen the doors to get you inside."

LeVar patted his abs. "I'll have you know that this is all muscle. Besides, I'm planning to start my food vlog, 'Eating Through Nightshade'. Gotta do thorough research, you know?"

“Are you seriously doing a vlog?” Scout asked.

“You know me. I’m full of surprises.” Before he could dive into his food, the phone buzzed inside his jacket. “It’s Thomas. I’ll take the call outside so I can hear better. Don’t nobody eat my mac-and-cheese.”

He eyed Raven, warning her not to steal his food like she used to when they were young. Had french fries been on the plate, they would already have disappeared.

On the sidewalk, the wind nipped at his exposed arms. He was wearing a T-shirt and hadn’t thought to put on a jacket.

"Hey, Shep Dawg. What's up?"

"LeVar, I have a situation. I need Wolf Lake Consulting to dive into an old case for me. It's serious."

LeVar leaned against the cold brick wall. "What kind of situation? Is this the Hannah Clarke disappearance?"

"Not just Hannah. We're looking at a series of kidnappings, going back decades. The pattern disturbs me, LeVar. It suggests we're dealing with a multiple-time offender."

The gravity of Thomas's words sank in. "A serial killer?"

"Potentially. My team is sitting on two decades' worth of conviction records from several prison databases and can't go through each criminal. I wouldn't ask if it wasn't important. We need to understand the pattern and see if there's a connection between the cases."

"You got it, Shep. I'll talk to Chelsey and Raven and get them on it," LeVar said, the gears already turning in his mind. "What if Scout and I approach the database from a technical perspective?"

"How so?"

"We're using advanced computing tools to sift through message forums on the Elliot Saunders investigation. No reason we can't do the same for the county."

"I owe you one."

"Nah. I owe you my life. That's more than enough payback."

Back inside, the mood at the table shifted as LeVar relayed the conversation.

Chelsey said, "We're still tracking Saunders' stalker. Can we manage both?"

Raven folded her arms. "We can't stretch ourselves thin. On the other hand, Thomas understands what we're up against and wouldn't ask if it wasn't critical."

"Agreed."

"Every time we help law enforcement solve a crime, it's another notch in our belt. WLC can always use the publicity."

LeVar laid out Thomas's request. "He's not asking us to solve the investigation alone. Just to help identify patterns and connections outside Nightshade County. The cases cross state lines, and the FBI is providing a profile. That will help. It's about pooling our resources and seeing the bigger picture."

The team fell into a thoughtful silence.

"I'll organize the workload to free up resources," Chelsey said.

"And I'll use machine learning to cross-reference cases across jurisdictions and identify similarities," Scout said.

LeVar smiled. "So it's settled. We'll help the sheriff's department, then catch Elliot Saunders' stalker."

Chelsey finished eating. "Ready when you are."

19

Thomas didn't like the sound the wind made when it moaned around the eaves. It reminded him of a person crying.

Night drenched the abandoned house in watery darkness. Only his flashlight lit the way. He stood at the window and peered down at the sidewalk. Several hours ago, a train of middle-school-age students had walked past. This was the perfect place from which to watch them.

He crouched and retrieved the discarded food wrapper with a pair of tweezers, Lambert by his side. Other than trespassing, no one had committed a crime here, but it never hurt to collect evidence. His instincts told him the kidnappings were starting again, though there was no proof to back up his intuition.

Thomas sealed the wrapper in a plastic evidence bag. "This isn't old," he said, examining the bag under the beam of his flashlight. "Could be from a few days ago, at most."

Lambert scanned the room, his own flashlight sweeping across the peeling wallpaper. "You think the kidnapper came here and used this place as a hideout?"

"More like an observation deck. Yeah, it's possible." Thomas dusted off his hands. "Or it could just be kids messing around. But given what we're digging into, we can't ignore any leads."

He led the way through the dilapidated house cautiously to avoid the debris scattered across the floor.

"Let's canvass the area," Thomas said. "I want to know if any of the neighbors noticed anything unusual. Lights in the windows, maybe someone coming and going." They descended the stairs. He stopped at the front door. "And I want a proper lock on this place. It's too easy for people to break in."

Lambert nodded, following Thomas out to the sidewalk. "I'll take the south side. You want to start from the north?"

"Sounds like a plan. Meet me back here in thirty."

As Thomas approached the first neighbor's house, he rehearsed the questions in his mind, ready to switch from the role of an investigator to a reassuring presence in the community. The balance was delicate but necessary, especially when fear could spread as quickly as facts.

Thomas rang the doorbell at the first house, a well-kept bungalow with a hedgerow along the sidewalk. The porch light turned on. A middle-aged woman opened the door, a cautious curiosity in her stance.

"Evening, ma'am. Sheriff Thomas Shepherd." He flashed his badge. "We're conducting a quick check in the neighborhood. Mind if I ask you a few questions?"

The woman's expression turned thoughtful. "Of course, Sheriff. What's this about?"

"We're looking into reports of unusual activity around the old Sorenson place. Have you noticed anything odd in the last few days? Maybe lights or someone around the property?"

She looked toward the abandoned house. "Now that you mention it, I did see something. Two nights ago, I noticed a light moving inside the house. Looked like a flashlight. I thought it might be kids playing around, but it was late."

Thomas scribbled a note. "Did you see anyone enter or leave the house?"

"No, I didn't. Just the light. It moved from one room to another and then went out. I've seen nothing since."

"Suspicious vehicles?"

"No, sir. But if I notice anyone, I'll call the department."

"Thank you, ma'am. That's very helpful. We're making sure the area stays safe."

"I appreciate you checking on this."

As Thomas walked away, he mulled over the new information. The light in the house might have belonged to the person who'd left the food wrapper. Whether it was a curious teenager or someone with more sinister intentions, he couldn't be sure. But it was a lead, and right now any lead was worth following up on.

After knocking on doors for another thirty minutes, he came away with no new information. He met Lambert back at the cruiser. His deputy had experienced a similar run of bad luck.

"We'll head to the station and hand this over to the lab," Thomas said, patting the evidence bag.

Back at the sheriff's office, the atmosphere switched to focused determination as Thomas laid out the plan for leveraging Wolf Lake Consulting's expertise. Emma was here with Aguilar and Lambert. They listened as Thomas detailed the approach to cross-referencing decades of cold cases.

Lambert shared his observations on the kidnapper's methodical selection of victims and locations, suggesting a pattern that could have evolved over time. "If we look at the geographic spread and timing between abductions, there might be a trail we missed," he said, pointing to a map on the wall marked with pins.

Aguilar said, "We need to consider the changes in technology and public awareness over the years. What was easy for him back then might have forced him to adapt his methods."

"That's assuming he's still active," Thomas said.

"We must consider the possibility."

He feared Aguilar was right.

Emma observed without participating in the discussion. Thomas watched her, mindful of the pain this conversation resurrected. As far as the journalist knew, this was a kidnapping case, not a murder investigation. Whenever the dialogue veered too close to the raw reality of what they were facing, he steered it back to the technical aspects of their investigation.

"I've spoken with the team at Wolf Lake Consulting," Thomas said. "They're ready to assist with analysis of the criminal database. They have the tools and expertise to sift through the information faster than we can."

The mention of Wolf Lake Consulting sparked a renewed sense of purpose among the team. The collaboration meant access to resources and analytical capabilities that had been beyond their reach.

"We're searching for patterns in the kidnappings," Thomas continued. "Anything we uncover needs to go to our contact at the BAU."

Emma finally spoke. "I want to help. Hannah deserves justice, as do the other girls."

"We'll take everything you can give us."

After discussing the investigation's new direction, Thomas called Erik Heden, his media contact in Syracuse. The newscaster, familiar with Thomas's dedication to law enforcement and community safety, recognized the importance of continuing to report on the cold cases.

"We'll run a special segment," Heden assured him. "The public needs to be reminded, and who knows? Maybe someone out there holds the key to solving these disappearances."

Once the call ended, Emma approached Thomas and his deputies with a photo album in her arms. She placed the collection on the table with a careful, almost reverential touch. Thomas noticed the tremble in her hands.

"These are pictures I saved of Hannah," Emma said, her voice catching.

Thomas removed a photo from its sleeve. The two smiling girls, frozen in a moment of innocent joy, drew his eyes. The depth of Emma's loss struck him. Not just her best friend, but her childhood, her past, were irrevocably altered by tragedy. Then he recognized the second girl in the picture. It was Emma.

The journalist pointed to the younger version of herself. "We were inseparable," she said. "I want people to remember Hannah like this. Happy and caring."

Thomas shared a look with his deputies. "We'll make sure they do." He glanced at the ceiling in thought. "You know what this community needs? A vigil."

"Not only will a vigil honor Hannah and the other girls," Aguilar said, "but it will get the investigation more attention."

"Without question," said Lambert.

They tossed around ideas. Aguilar added logistics for crowd control.

"This is about bringing closure to the families," Thomas said.

Lambert, already on the phone, coordinated with community leaders, securing the village square for the event. "We'll need candles, a PA system, and I'm thinking of inviting the high school choir. They won the state championship."

Emma expressed her willingness to speak at the vigil. "It's time I did more than just remember Hannah from behind the scenes."

Her decision to share her story publicly marked a significant step, one that Thomas admired for its bravery and its potential to touch the hearts of the gatherers.

"If you don't mind," Emma said, "I'll head back to the hotel and start on my speech. Bright and early tomorrow morning?"

"We'll be here," Thomas said. After the door closed, he pulled Aguilar aside. "Monitor Emma during the event. If our suspect is still around, the vigil will draw him out."

Aguilar squared her shoulders. "Don't worry. Lambert and I will stay ready. The killer won't get anywhere near Emma."

20

LeVar was an hour into his work at Wolf Lake Consulting when Scout entered the office and set her backpack beside her desk. The pink in her cheeks suggested she'd run here after school released for the day.

"Where are you on the Hannah Clarke case?" she asked, tossing her hair over one shoulder.

This was the way he wanted their relationship to stay—friends only. Anything more would be terribly wrong. He did his best not to meet her eyes.

"I loaded over a hundred convicted criminals into a cloud database."

"That many?" she said, shocked.

"Keep in mind the database covers a few dozen correctional facilities between here and Northern Pennsylvania. I even tossed in a few from Western New England, since two girls disappeared between Albany and the Massachusetts border. Can you help me make sense of the data?"

"Shove over."

When she sat on his chair so they were hip to hip, he forced himself not to walk away. It was good that she was so comfortable around him, right? He pictured late-night study sessions at Kane Grove University. Maybe she would be eighteen then, and he would be twenty-two. The four-year age difference still seemed like a lot, but not as creepy as it did today. He shook his head to clear the thought away.

"You okay, LeVar?"

"Just thinking about college."

"I can't wait."

"Yeah, you told me. How did that physics exam go?"

Her face lit up, and she reached into her backpack. After she slapped the exam on the desk—she'd scored a perfect 100—he wanted to celebrate. But this meant there was no turning back. Before long, she would graduate early and join him at Kane Grove. He knew the university would accept her. Heck, they'd accepted him. Would they really turn away a straight-A, single-parent student who'd survived a crippling car accident and learned to walk again?

"Looks like you'll have company at college."

He swung his dreadlocks to the side. "Bet."

Scout studied the extensive database LeVar had compiled. The screen before them came alive with rows of data, each entry representing a cold-blooded child predator who had operated during the last thirty years.

LeVar, leaning over to give Scout room, marveled at her skill. Someday, if all went as planned, he would be a grunt on the front line of a small-town police force. Or maybe he'd work as a low-level agent with the FBI if he was lucky. But Scout would work behind the scenes as a profiler with more computing skills than half of Silicon Valley. After she graduated, she could write her ticket.

"You're great at this," he commented, keeping the conversation professional.

"I had a great teacher," she replied without looking up, her attention fixed on the screen as the software began its analysis. Her words, meant to be light, clutched at LeVar's chest. He was more than her teacher; he was her friend, her mentor. And soon her college peer.

As the program churned through the data, identifying patterns of abduction and behavior, it flagged several child predators who had been active around the time of Hannah's disappearance. Many had histories of crossing state lines, making their tracking and capture more complicated.

"What do you see?"

"Look at this one." She pointed to a profile on the screen. "He was arrested in Vermont but was suspected in cases in New York and Pennsylvania. Right around when Hannah vanished."

LeVar scrutinized the details Scout highlighted.

"And here," he said, pointing to another line. "This one was caught in Massachusetts but had lived in Albany. We should mark him for a deeper dive."

"Totally."

"You notice anything about the girls these two targeted?"

"They're all between the ages of ten and thirteen."

"You hit the mark," he said. "Either of these guys could be our unsub."

She tapped a nail against the column on the far right. "The system flagged both for still being incarcerated."

"That's a good thing. We'll find more like these guys. Keep searching."

Together they compiled a list of suspects whose crimes mirrored the circumstances of Hannah's case. Each name added to their list was a potential lead.

"It's like looking for a needle in a haystack, but the needle is moving, and so is the haystack."

LeVar smirked at her analogy. "I've never seen a moving

haystack, but okay. We're making progress. This could lead us to Hannah's killer."

Raven and Chelsey scooted over in their chairs as Scout and LeVar continued their analysis.

"What have you got?" Raven asked.

LeVar gestured at the screen. "Two dozen criminals who might have kidnapped and murdered Hannah Clarke. These guys were active in the Northeastern U.S. around the same time she vanished."

Chelsey set an elbow on the desk. "Let's cross-reference their methodologies with what we know about Hannah's disappearance."

Working as a cohesive unit, they uncovered a disturbing trend of abductions that spanned several states. Scout's software proved invaluable, highlighting overlooked connections that now seemed glaringly obvious.

Raven's analytical skills and Chelsey's methodical approach complemented LeVar's knowledge and Scout's technical prowess.

Finally, LeVar compiled their findings into a comprehensive report. "We have sixteen names here. Twelve are in prison. The other four are loose. Any of these guys could be the unsub, but we've narrowed the list enough for Thomas, Lambert, and Aguilar to figure out who the killer is."

Chelsey looked over his shoulder. "This is solid work, LeVar and Scout. I'm glad you completed the task so quickly. Remember, we have our hands full with the Elliot Saunders case. We can't lose focus."

Raven agreed. "Let's mail this over to Thomas. He needs to see it. But after that, it's back to Saunders. That investigation won't solve itself."

With one click, LeVar sent the report to Thomas. As the

email disappeared into the digital ether, he hoped they had done enough to help the sheriff.

"All right, all right. We have just enough time to—"

The ringing phone cut Chelsey short.

"Wolf Lake Consulting," she said. After a brief conversation, she placed the caller on speakerphone.

It was Elliot Saunders. He sounded different this time; the confidence in his tone had been replaced by anxiety.

"You were right," Saunders said. "I treated the harassment as an annoyance instead of a genuine threat. But I can't anymore."

"What happened, Mr. Saunders?" Raven asked.

The AI specialist spoke of odd occurrences: the sensation of someone following him, items disappearing from his residence and workplace, and a shadowed figure trailing him through Harmon and Syracuse. Each account added layers of concern to the team. The stalker was escalating.

LeVar's expression turned grave. "We're taking this seriously. This isn't online harassment anymore. He's stalking you in the physical world, so we need to adapt our approach."

Raven jumped into the conversation. "Mr. Saunders, we'll walk you through enhancing your home security. We can also set up routine surveillance missions. But you need to remain as vigilant as possible. Let's set up a plan for you to check in with us every few hours throughout the day."

After the call ended, Chelsey took the lead and strategized their next moves. She organized the team's resources, integrating Saunders' latest information into their investigation. The shift was immediate and all-encompassing. Their task was twofold: ensure Saunders's safety and adapt their investigative techniques to this new, more dangerous phase of the stalker's campaign.

"I told you this would happen," Raven said.

LeVar set his chin on steepled fingers. "No arguments. How do you want to handle this?"

"I'm uncomfortable with Saunders hopping from conference to conference with nobody to watch his back."

"You think we should follow him?"

"As much as time allows. We're only three investigators, and we can't expect Scout to join us in the field."

The teenager appeared disappointed, but it was ludicrous to expect the girl to carry a gun and protect a millionaire. Heck, even LeVar wasn't old enough to become an official private investigator. His deputy position with the Nightshade County Sheriff's Department allowed him to circumvent New York State's rules.

"First things first," said Chelsey. "Items disappeared from his workplace and home. It's possible Saunders misplaced them, but I doubt it. He needs a foolproof security system."

"I'll make a call," Raven said.

LeVar shared a look with Scout. They needed to track the stalker's IP address and identify him before it was too late.

21

Thomas hoped to arrive home before Chelsey and surprise her with dinner, but her Honda Civic was sitting in the driveway when he pulled up to the lakeside home. After working late the last few days, he'd given himself a break today and left the station on time. The mayor had scheduled the vigil for this coming Friday night, which gave him a few more days to work out any snags and ensure his deputies kept Emma safe.

Jack was the first to greet Thomas inside. The gigantic dog set its paws on his chest and licked his face.

"Are you the same pup who was afraid to come out of the brush?" he asked.

Thomas had discovered Jack on the trail leading up to the state park when the dog was a third of its current size. Would he grow larger? Pretty soon, the house would be too small for the wolflike canine.

He'd barely hung his coat when Chelsey emerged from the living room, a sheaf of papers in hand. The A-frame's open layout allowed the late-day light to filter through. She hadn't started cooking. Good. He pulled ingredients from the fridge.

"I saw your car in the drive," Thomas said, setting a pot on the stove. "How was your day?"

Chelsey set the papers on the kitchen island and sighed. "Eventful. We ramped up security for Elliot Saunders, and we spent time on your serial kidnapping case. It's all hands on deck now."

"Thanks for the help. It means a lot."

He moved around the kitchen, choosing the perfect spices from the cupboard. As he chopped vegetables and plopped them into a pot, the room filled with the aroma of cooking. The activity grounded him and helped him forget the horrors he faced every day.

"So," she said, resting her back against the counter, "I was thinking about the wedding. Maybe we could start looking at invitations?"

The question hung in the air, mingling with the scent of garlic and onions. A frown creased his forehead. "Yeah, of course. Invitations."

Chelsey noticed the shift in his demeanor and the way his hands stilled over the cutting board. "Hey, if it's too much right now, we can figure it out later. I just thought . . ."

"No, no, you're right." He set aside the knife. "Let's talk about the wedding. I want it to be perfect."

"It will be. But it's okay to take it one step at a time. How about we start with something simple? Like the color scheme?"

"Sounds good. Maybe something aqua blue? That was your favorite color in high school."

She touched his cheek and planted a kiss on his lips. "Still is. Thank you for remembering."

"All right, we'll work on the invitations after dinner."

"Really?"

"I promise."

She kissed him again.

He wouldn't let her down, though the prospect of writing invitations all night made him tense. They would have to settle on a guest list, and that was the worst part. Who to invite? Who to leave off the list? He didn't want the pressure or to disappoint anyone.

As they ate, the wedding plans were always in his thoughts, as tangible as the steam rising from their dinner plates.

Chelsey, ever the perceptive partner, dialed back the pressure with a suggestion that lit a path Thomas felt he could navigate.

"Let's just concentrate on writing the invitations. We'll decide later who should come."

"So we'll throw away some invitations?"

"That's my thinking."

Thomas wanted a small, intimate ceremony, fearing a larger event would overwhelm them. But disappointing Chelsey was the last thing he wanted to do.

After clearing the dinner table together, they washed and dried the plates. Jack's larger-than-life presence followed them like a shadow that craved leftovers. His snout nudged Thomas's leg. Then he sat with his tail thumping the floor.

"Okay, boy. I'll feed you next." He noticed Tigger entering the room. "And you."

Thomas and Chelsey settled in the living room with the box of invitations between them.

"I'll take everyone on my side of the family," she said.

"And I'll handle my family."

The first person to invite was easy. Mother. Except that he didn't know what to write once he drew a comma after her name. Would he write the wrong words and offend her? No, that was silly. She loved Thomas and Chelsey and would come no matter how clunky his writing was.

It wasn't long before Jack's curiosity got the better of him.

The dog sniffed around the box, his nose brushing against the paper.

"Go get your bone," Chelsey said.

Jack pawed at the invitations, as if to say he wanted to be part of the process. Tigger, the opportunist, joined the fray, attracted by the rustling papers and dangling ribbons.

"These aren't cat toys," Thomas said.

Tigger didn't seem to care.

Chelsey laughed. "Look at these two, plotting their next caper."

Thomas picked up a pen, ready to write the next invitation. They would invite LeVar, Raven, and their mother Serena. Another simple decision that required no thought. He got to work.

Chelsey clamped a pen between her teeth. "Naomi and Scout are definitely invited."

"Hundred percent."

She glanced up. "You got that saying from LeVar."

"He rubs off on me."

They sealed their first set of invitations. Then Jack, with a playful gleam in his eye, snatched the box of invitations and took off like a shot.

"Jack, no!" Chelsey called.

His paws clacked against the floorboards as the dog ran into the kitchen. Chelsey's surprised shout and Thomas skidding around a corner added to the hilarity.

The chase wound through the house, under tables, around chairs, a merry dance of humans and dog. Jack seemed to relish the attention and the thrill of the game. Just when they thought they had him cornered, Jack would dart away, the box clutched in his jaws, his tail wagging in delight.

Now they were on the second floor. Jack set the box in the

hallway, poised over his toy. With a woof, he dared Thomas to take it away.

"You're not helping things, Jack," Thomas said.

Inwardly, he appreciated the dog for rescuing him from the invitations. Chelsey glared at him as if she suspected he'd put Jack up to this.

"The game is over," Chelsey said. "Jack, give us the invitations."

Another woof.

Thomas approached with caution. At any moment, Jack would snatch the box and sprint past them. The dog was much too fast for him to catch.

Chelsey fanned out to the side, as if blocking the corridor would stop the dog from escaping. Fat chance.

"Jack," Thomas said. He put bass in his voice. "I'm not fooling around. Give us the box."

The dog looked from Thomas to Chelsey, then sat back on his haunches.

"Good boy." Chelsey retrieved the invitations and petted the dog's head. "Thank you for cooperating. I promise we'll play after Mommy and Daddy work."

Mommy and Daddy. Thomas had never felt closer to Chelsey and couldn't wait until they were married.

That was when the shredding sounds came from downstairs.

"The envelopes!" Chelsey and Thomas yelled in unison.

They rushed down the stairs and found the once pristine envelopes shredded. Tigger batted tiny fragments of paper across the floorboards.

"Tigger, don't," Chelsey said.

But it was already too late. The cat had even destroyed the invitations they'd written. The sight was so absurd that their frustration melted into laughter.

"Why do we let animals live in our house?" Chelsey asked.

Tigger, satisfied with his contribution, sauntered off with a flick of his tail.

Sorting through the aftermath, Thomas and Chelsey separated salvageable invitations from the casualties.

"How many did we lose?"

"Eight out of ten."

He assessed the remaining envelopes. "Ha, he didn't eat the invitations to my mother or LeVar."

"Oh, you think your work is done for the night?"

"No, but I'm two ahead of you."

"Are you challenging me to a race, Thomas Shepherd?"

He clicked a pen. "It's on."

22

The first light of day hadn't broken when Thomas arrived at the station. Lambert and Aguilar were scheduled to start their shifts at seven, but both deputies were already there. With a shrug of his shoulders, he passed their vehicles in the parking lot. Nobody worked harder than his crew.

He claimed three letters from Maggie's desk and carried them to his office. Lambert was chatting with a deputy from the graveyard shift. They discussed the candidates Wolf Lake Consulting had emailed to the department.

Thomas placed a hand on the exhausted deputy's arm. "Head home. You need rest."

"But there's another hour left on my shift," the man said.

"Don't worry about it. I'm here now, and so are Lambert and Aguilar."

"Thanks, Sheriff. I won't forget this."

Thomas smiled. He knew how difficult the midnight shift was. Staying up all night wasn't natural unless you were a vampire.

Aguilar met him outside the kitchen with a strange-looking

smoothie in her hand. She approached with a smirk and extended a mason jar. The concoction was an unsettling shade of green. "Morning, Thomas. You'll need this today."

Thomas eyed the smoothie. "What's in it?"

"Just try it. Trust me, it's packed with everything you need to get through the day."

With resignation, Thomas took the jar and braced himself for the worst. The first sip surprised him; it was tangy and somewhat sweet, far from the dreadful taste he'd expected.

"Not bad, but it looks like nuclear waste. Are you sure this is good for me?"

Aguilar couldn't contain her grin. "It's kale, spinach, ginger, apple, and a few other superfoods. Oh, and a spoonful of spirulina for an extra kick."

Thomas stopped mid-sip, the word *spirulina* giving him pause. "I'm drinking algae?"

"See? You liked it before you knew what it was. Mind over matter."

Lambert walked over and raised an eyebrow at the green residue around Thomas's mouth. "What's got you looking like a health nut, boss man?"

Thomas wiped his lips and shot a mock glare at Aguilar. "Just trying to survive the day."

Lambert chuckled. "Well, if we're done with the morning's culinary adventures, I have a few calls to make. We've got a lot of ground to cover if we're going to coordinate with other jurisdictions about these kidnapping cases."

"Let's get to it. Aguilar, can you reach out to your contacts? We'll need to cast a wide net."

"No problem," she said. "I'll start with the counties closest to ours and work my way out. That good with you, Lambert?"

The tall deputy nodded. "That will free me up to handle the out-of-state jurisdictions."

Before Thomas could follow Lambert, Aguilar grabbed his arm. "We should talk."

"About?"

She lowered her voice and assessed him through the top of her eyes. "Thomas, I know you're convinced a convict took Hannah Clarke."

"You disagree?"

"I went over the timeline and the old witness statements, and I kept coming back to Nolan Trevino."

The curious man on the spectrum. "Nolan Trevino wouldn't harm a hair on a child's head."

"After Trevino died, the kidnappings stopped."

"That proves nothing."

"But we have eyewitnesses who place him in the park on numerous occasions. Everybody claims he would sit on the bench and watch the children play."

"So do plenty of people, and we don't suspect they're child predators," he said.

A hurt expression came over her face. "I don't want to believe Trevino killed Hannah Clarke, but you have to consider the possibility."

He exhaled. "Okay, I'll speak with his family."

"That's all I ask, Thomas. Check every box. The sooner we eliminate Trevino from the suspect list, the happier we'll be."

He didn't dispute her logic. Nolan's name had haunted him since entering the discussion. Thomas knew what it was like to be different. People whispered about you and passed judgment.

An hour later, he stopped his cruiser in front of Daphne Trevino's house. She was Nolan's younger sister and about the same age as Thomas. Would she remember him from school?

He straightened his uniform before approaching the front door. The middle-class neighborhood was quiet. Daphne's house, modest and well-kept, blended into a row of similar two-story designs.

He rang the bell and waited, rehearsing questions in his mind. He needed to be delicate with this inquiry. Nolan Trevino's name brought up painful memories for many in Wolf Lake, not least for his family.

The door opened and Daphne stood before him. Time had touched her gently, her features soft but defined, a mirror of her brother's in many ways. Recognition sparked in her eyes.

"Thomas Shepherd. How long has it been?"

"Hello, Daphne. I hope I'm not intruding. I have a few questions about Nolan, if you have a moment."

She stepped aside and invited him in. "The news is talking about that kidnapped girl again. I wondered when the police would come asking about Nolan." Her tone sounded resigned and sad.

They sat, and Thomas took a moment to observe the surroundings. Photographs filled the house, many of Nolan, showcasing his life and the people in it.

“I'm revisiting Hannah Clarke's case. Your brother's name came up in the investigation.”

“I understand. He was an easy target for suspicion. Different, but not dangerous. You, of all people, should know how unfairly the village treated him.”

“I do. Believe me, I only want to clear his name and catch the real kidnapper. What can you tell me about your brother?”

She set her hands on her knees. “He loved this town and the children in it. He would watch them play. I think it was because he lived vicariously through them. Kids wanted nothing to do with him when he was a child. It breaks my heart.”

"Trust me, I understand. Did Nolan ever mention Hannah Clarke?"

"Only after she disappeared. Nolan often lost himself in his own world, but Hannah's kidnapping hurt him, like it did all of us."

"What else can you tell me? Why were people so convinced that your brother kidnapped Hannah?"

"We gave him a video camera one year," Daphne said, her voice laced with nostalgia. "He was so proud of it. Nolan would take it to the park and film the kids playing. But that only raised suspicions."

Thomas tensed, the mention of the video camera setting off alarm bells in his mind. Filming children in the park? He understood why so many people thought he was a predator.

"What did he do with these videotapes?"

"He would watch them in his room. And before you get any sick ideas in your head, it wasn't like that. He would pretend to be one of them."

"Are you positive?"

"Nolan just wanted to be part of their world, to experience the joy and freedom he'd never had. He always felt he'd missed out on his own childhood."

Thomas pondered her words, trying to reconcile the image of a man ostracized for his differences with the potential implications of his actions.

"Did you keep the recordings?"

He hated asking, but it was necessary.

"Yes. I kept everything. Nolan was a collector of moments. Would you like to see them? I still have the tapes. They're in a box in his closet."

Thomas didn't need to inquire whether she'd kept Nolan's room exactly as it was before he died. Viewing the recordings could either exonerate the man or raise additional questions. "Yes, I would appreciate that, Daphne. It will help with my investigation."

As Daphne disappeared into another room to retrieve the

tapes, Thomas couldn't help but feel conflicted. The idea of Nolan Trevino, a man known for his gentleness, harming a child seemed far-fetched. Yet he'd learned that the truth was often stranger than fiction.

Daphne returned with the box of videotapes. There had to be a dozen inside.

"Here you are. You'll keep them safe?"

"I'll guard them with my life."

A tear crept out of her eye.

"I knew you would. Clear my brother's name, Thomas."

23

At his workstation, LeVar directed the rotating fan so it blew across him and Scout. With so many computers running, the main office often overheated and became uncomfortable. The only issue was that the artificial wind blew papers off his desk if he didn't weigh them down.

Scout was working on the heuristics program. Across the room, Raven chewed her lip, then closed her eyes and yanked on her braided hair.

"Beating yourself up again, sis?"

She gave him a level stare. "I'm a tad frustrated."

"About what?"

"It's this schedule. Between monitoring Saunders and working on other cases, we don't have enough bodies to cover our shifts."

"What about Darren? Can he help?"

Darren Holt, a former Syracuse police officer, was the ranger at Wolf Lake State Park and Raven's boyfriend. LeVar considered the ranger one of his best friends, but he hadn't seen the man in weeks. This was the busiest time of the year for Darren.

"He would in a heartbeat, but spring weather is right around the corner. All week, he's cleaning the trails and making sure everything is ready for the hikers."

"Bet. Why don't you give me more hours? It's not like you're paying me."

She grinned. "True, but you have class and your deputy job to worry about. Since Scout is our technology specialist and doesn't work in the field, it's down to me, you, and Chelsey. We should have enough people to cover our shifts, but I can't make it work."

"I'm still putting in thirty to forty hours a week at WLC. That should be enough, yeah?"

"It should be," Raven said, massaging her temples. "Why can't I figure out this schedule?"

Chelsey, who had engrossed herself in Elliot Saunders' background, looked up from her computer without responding.

"Scout, can you minimize the heuristics search and let it run in the background?" he asked.

"Absolutely," the girl said.

"Check it. I'm about to solve all your problems, sis."

Raven frowned. "Yeah, I'll believe it when I see it. I've been over this schedule six ways from Sunday, and I can't make it work. Either we have too many people or not enough. And then there are your college classes to think about, plus Scout's school schedule."

"Roll that chair over so I can drop some knowledge on you."

Raven didn't appear convinced, but she did as he requested. "Okay, impress me."

He opened an AI application that displayed a blinking cursor as it awaited his prompt. "First, I'll tell the software what days and hours I'm available."

"Will it remember?"

"Sure." He entered the data, and the application prompted him for more information. "Next, let's tell the software about your schedule, then Chelsey's. We won't include Darren, since he's a longshot to help over the next week."

Interested, Raven shifted her chair closer. "I have Elliot Saunders' meetings schedule. Want that as well?"

"Definitely."

LeVar tapped the Enter key and initiated the AI's scheduling algorithm. They all watched the screen, even Chelsey, who had abandoned her workstation to see what the fuss was all about.

"Come on, come on," Raven said. "This had better work."

The AI software processed the schedules, commitments, and constraints. The screen refreshed, presenting an organized timetable.

"Would you look at that?" LeVar asked, tapping himself on the shoulder with pride. "Every shift covered, Saunders watched over, and we even have overlapping coverage for extra security."

Raven leaned closer, her earlier skepticism replaced by amazement. "And it even slotted in downtime. I didn't think that was possible with our workload."

Chelsey chuckled. "I don't know if I should be impressed or terrified. What did you say to this thing?"

"I just asked nicely," LeVar said. "And maybe promised it a sandwich."

Raven rolled her eyes. "Fine, I'll head over to The Broken Yolk in a few. But this thing better not get used to special treatment."

Scout asked, "Does this mean I get more time for my software updates and debugging?"

LeVar studied the schedule. "Looks like it. You have dedicated blocks for tech work."

"Awesome sauce."

The team spent a few minutes going over the new schedule, adjusting to the AI's recommendations. LeVar explained the logic behind some of the more intricate scheduling decisions, ensuring everyone was comfortable and confident with the plan.

"So, we're all good?" Raven asked, looking around the table. "This new schedule works for everyone?"

“It works,” Chelsey said, “but this technology scares the heck out of me.”

"I hear you, Chelsey. As much as I appreciate what AI can do, it kinda freaks me out."

LeVar raised his palms. "Freaks you out? In what way?"

"It's the privacy thing, for starters. There's always a machine watching and analyzing your every move. It's a bit much."

Chelsey squinted at the screen. "I'm with Raven on this. There's something cold and impersonal about relying on AI for everything. It makes you wonder if there'll come a day when we're more machine than human."

LeVar considered their points. "I get where you're coming from. The privacy aspect is definitely something to be cautious about. But think about the time it saved us, the efficiency it's brought to our work."

“Efficiency is great, don't get me wrong. But where do we draw the line? At what point does it stop being a tool and become a crutch?”

Raven added, "And what about the jobs it could replace? There's a whole debate out there about AI taking over roles that humans fill. Imagine a world without a human touch."

“I doubt it will ever come to that,” he said. “Maybe the key is finding a balance and using AI to handle the mundane, repetitive tasks while keeping the more sensitive, nuanced work in human hands.”

“What if the machines decide they want to handle more?”

That was an unsettling thought. "You think Saunders' stalker is one of those AI-phobics?"

Scout swiped through her tablet, looking at online new articles. "It's possible. There have been protests in major cities, some turning violent. People are scared of what AI represents for the future."

Raven peered over Scout's shoulder. "Fear can drive people to extreme actions. If Saunders is the face of AI advancement, it's not a stretch to think someone might target him."

"So, we're looking for someone with a strong aversion to AI," Chelsey said. "Maybe someone who is vocal in these forums or attended these protests."

Scout ran an internet search and loaded a forum. "I've seen heated discussions on this one. Some people are concerned about job loss, but others are militant in their opposition."

"If your theory is correct, that narrows down our profile," LeVar said. "Someone who's not just technophobic but engaging in anti-AI rhetoric. Possibly someone who's had a negative experience with tech in the past."

"And if they're part of a group, there might be a trail we can follow. Group memberships, online postings, maybe even public incidents at protests," Raven added.

"I'm not convinced, yo. Something tells me this guy is a more than technophobic. He's a rival." LeVar swiveled back and forth in his chair. "We need to get ahead of this guy and think like he does. Saunders might have made enemies in the past, right? We should reach out to him and press him about rivals. Don't accept his story that he gets along with everyone."

"We all have enemies."

"Batman has the Joker, Hannibal Lecter has Dr. Chilton."

"And you have the empty donut box."

"Ha-ha."

Scout tapped a pen against her notebook. "That makes sense. Saunders has been in the AI field for years. There has to be someone consistently opposing him, not just these recent protesters."

"You're suggesting this is a man with a personal vendetta against Saunders?" Raven asked.

Though the profile was a work in progress, LeVar's confidence grew. "Think about it. The level of dedication, leaving messages, following Saunders from site to site. This isn't overnight hatred; this feels like it's been brewing for a while. Saunders needs to come clean. Either that or we let this stalker escalate. I'll talk to him. I think I can get him to see the urgency."

Chelsey jotted a note. "If you're right, LeVar, and this is a longtime rival, he might slip up trying to discredit Saunders. We can use that."

"I'll set up a meeting with Saunders as soon as possible. The sooner we get those names, the sooner we can catch this guy."

24

Thomas had tempered his expectations. How many people could he expect to attend a vigil honoring a girl who'd vanished so long ago?

Yet he was looking at an overflowing village square. Residents carried candles, and people crowded close to the stage, where he would speak before turning the microphone over to Emma. Even the journalist appeared surprised. She carried a picture of Hannah as she mingled with people who just wanted to express their condolences and thank her for planning this event.

"Hey, Thomas," Aguilar said, nudging him. "This is twice as many people as we expected."

"It's beautiful."

"Yes, but it will make keeping track of Emma more difficult. I realize everyone wants to speak to her, but perhaps we should keep her close. That is, if you believe the killer is still at large."

Nervous energy rolled through his body. Though he'd narrowed the prison database to several likely suspects, he worried Hannah's murderer had never gone away. But if the killer was here, why had he gone dormant for so long?

"Emma," he called.

The journalist turned toward his voice. "Sheriff?"

"Why don't you let Aguilar go over your speech?"

Anything to keep the woman close. He scanned the crowd. There were plenty of smiles and a few tears. Now and then, a face he didn't recognize caught his attention. He couldn't afford to become paranoid. The media had gotten the word out, and people had traveled from all over the county for this vigil. He should have expected to see unfamiliar faces.

The sun went down. Lights shone over the village square, but they weren't enough to scour away all the shadows. So many children lost. The possibility that the killer walked among the crowd made Thomas edgier than ever.

The sheriff filed through the crowd. Several hands touched his shoulder, and many thanked him for allowing them to gather. He acknowledged each, but kept one eye on the stage, where Emma rehearsed her lines with Aguilar. On the other side of the park, he glimpsed Lambert, who'd taken a strategic position on a rise overlooking the square. The tall deputy gave him a thumbs up, and Thomas returned the gesture.

When he returned to the stage, Emma was a whirlwind of anxiety. She was a writer, not an on-screen personality. Thomas doubted she'd ever spoken in front of this many observers. By his estimate, there were close to a thousand people crowding the square.

His breath formed clouds as he pulled his jacket together. "Ready?"

Emma bounced on her heels and rattled the papers. "Ready as I'll ever be. Deputy Aguilar says it's an excellent speech."

"I'm sure it is." He glanced at Aguilar, who winked. "Remember the plan. Deliver the speech, and make eye contact with the crowd. If anyone frightens you or makes an aggressive move toward the stage, alert us immediately."

"I understand."

"Aguilar will cover you. Lambert is across the way, and I'll handle crowd control near the podium. We have additional deputies stationed at the exits. Provided you remain alert, you're safe."

For the first time, Emma seemed to notice how close to the stage everyone was. Her shoulders stiffened.

"Aguilar," Thomas said, "help me move some of these people back."

His lead deputy joined him in clearing a path in front of the podium. A sound rose out of the crowd, and he realized people were singing. Had he not been responsible for keeping everybody safe, he might have sobbed. All these people with candles and tear-streaked faces. How many had lost a child because of one madman?

A commotion in the crowd made Thomas's head turn. He lifted his radio. "Lambert, what's happening at my ten o'clock?"

"TV news reporter," Lambert said through the speaker. "It's that Vance Talbot from the Binghamton news station."

Thomas's stomach turned over. Talbot was aggressive and vying for a big-city news job. He thought nothing of stepping on people to get what he wanted. Now he pushed through the crowd with an assistant, who used his shoulder-mounted camera as a battering ram to clear a path.

"He's going to trample someone. Can you intervene?"

"Heading that way now."

Too late. Talbot and his assistant had pushed their way to the stage. Groans from the crowd didn't dissuade the reporter. He wanted his story and would get it, no matter who he injured.

Vance Talbot zeroed in on Emma. He threw questions at her, each one more insensitive than the last.

"Emma, we learned that you abandoned Hannah Clarke on the day she disappeared. What do you have to say about that?"

Emma stammered as the camera zoomed in on her face.

"How do you feel, knowing Hannah's abductor might never be found?"

With her face a mask of strained composure, she attempted to deflect. "Tonight is about remembering Hannah and the other missing children, not speculating."

"But if you hadn't left Hannah alone, she might still be alive. That must horrify you."

Unable to reach the steps, Thomas climbed onto the stage. He caught Lambert's eye and nodded towards the journalist. Lambert and Aguilar moved in, positioning themselves between Talbot and Emma.

"Off the stage," Thomas said. "Now."

The camera swung to the sheriff.

"Why?" Talbot asked. "Do you have something to hide, Sheriff? I understand Nolan Trevino, a man you've defended, might be the killer."

The crowd shifted uneasily. Whispers grew into murmurs of disapproval.

Stepping forward, Thomas raised his hand for silence. "I apologize for the interruption. Tonight, we gather not for sensational stories but to remember those we've lost and to stand together in hope and solidarity." His gaze swept over the crowd, meeting eyes, offering reassurance.

Lambert, with a strong and insistent hand, guided Talbot away from the stage, suggesting a more appropriate time and place for his inquiries. Aguilar remained close to Emma.

The crowd settled, the earlier harmony restored as Thomas continued. "Let's remind ourselves why we're here. To honor memories, to share our strength, and to light the way forward with love and remembrance."

In the background, Talbot stomped away with his camera operator trailing behind.

A hush fell as Emma approached the podium. The air, crisp with the onset of evening, seemed to hold its breath along with the crowd. Thomas stationed himself in view of Emma and Talbot, who observed from afar.

Clearing her throat, Emma tapped the microphone.

"We gather here not just to remember Hannah," she said, "but to affirm our commitment to all our missing children. Hannah dreamed of becoming a journalist, to tell stories that mattered. She is why I do what I do; I pray she is proud."

Emma's tribute flowed. She weaved personal anecdotes with a call to never forget. Thomas could almost feel the resolve growing in the square. These tragedies would never happen again.

As she began to speak, the sound system emitted a shriek. Several people covered their ears. Thomas looked toward the sound operator, who threw up his hands in disbelief.

A discordant voice followed. Thomas spun around, searching for the source of the attack. He swore he heard Hannah's name beneath the static.

He rushed to the sound booth. As he ran, he scanned the sea of faces for any hint of the culprit. The murmurs of the crowd, a mix of confusion and rising panic, underscored the urgency of the situation.

"Stay calm," he called as he passed through the people.

Reaching the technical area, he found the staff checking cables and settings, their faces a picture of bafflement.

"What happened?" Thomas asked.

"We don't know, Sheriff," the lead technician replied. "Everything was fine. It's like someone hijacked the system."

Aguilar's voice came through the radio. "Perimeter's secure, Thomas. Nobody's leaving without a check."

"Good. Keep it tight," Thomas said.

He watched as the sound crew adjusted the mixer's levels. Someone had manipulated their equipment.

Thomas's thoughts turned dark. As the technical team worked to reset the system, the sheriff knew this was an attack on the community's resolve. The saboteur wanted to instill fear.

With Aguilar and Lambert maintaining a watchful eye on the crowd, Thomas returned to Emma, who trembled and darted her eyes from face to face.

"You're safe now," he said.

"He's here," Emma said. "I can feel him."

25

Code scrolling down a screen. The black of night waiting outside the window.

That's what Elliot Saunders saw as he troubleshooted his new artificial intelligence creation. This was the breakthrough that would make everyone sit up and take notice. He wasn't to be underestimated. Not after he brought his new technology to the world.

A row of security monitors lined the wall beside his desk. From his chair, he could view the yard, the street, and several rooms inside his house. He had to hand it to the investigators at Wolf Lake Consulting. They'd set him up with a topnotch home security firm. The house was like a fortress.

He opened a second window and compared more code with the troubleshooting results. So close. All he needed to do was find a bug, and he could bring this code to the artificial intelligence community.

A security camera flickered. That was unusual. The system was brand new. Nothing should malfunction. He narrowed his eyes as the monitor reset. The screen showed the lawn outside his bedroom window. Nobody was outside.

On the street, a car sped past. He returned to his work.

The phone ringing made him jump. When he picked up, nobody replied to his voice. He slammed the phone against the table and concentrated on the task at hand. No more interruptions.

A buzzing sound came from the security system. What was happening? If the system failed, he'd demand the installer come out and fix it. Immediately. When you paid this much for security, you expected results, not excuses.

He crouched behind the monitors and checked the cables. All fastened. No frayed wires.

Sitting down, he surveyed every screen and ensured he was alone. Ever since the shadowy figure had started following him between his work and various speaking engagements, he'd become paranoid.

But nobody showed up on the monitors, and the green lights on the security system told him the house was locked down and safe.

When he picked up the mouse, the screen that had flickered went black.

"You have to be kidding me."

He would raise hell with the installer. This was unacceptable.

With a whack against the side of the monitor, he attempted to get it working again. He should have known that would fail.

Then another monitor went black. And a third.

Saunders drew in a breath. He could no longer see what was happening inside or outside his house.

The code on his screen began disappearing.

"No!"

He typed as the commands disappeared, but he wasn't fast enough. Someone was deleting his code.

Impossible. Nobody could hack into his private network.

But it was happening.

He turned his attention back to the screen. An application evaporated. All the work he'd completed over the last month—gone. This was a disaster. He was ruined.

Dialing the firm who'd installed his system, he spoke to a disinterested-sounding woman who promised to send someone out to check his monitors tomorrow morning.

"What about now? My code. It's disappearing!"

"Mr. Saunders, our company doesn't handle private networks. If you'd like me to refer you to someone who can help . . ."

He hung up before she could continue. Worthless.

On the computer screen, more code vanished, as if consumed by an invisible being. An idea formed in his head. Unplug the computers and network servers. Kill the power.

But was it too late to save his masterpiece?

He ran from one surge protector to the next, turning off each. Computers and servers powered down. Silence crept into the room.

With nobody left to help, he called Wolf Lake Consulting. It was late, but maybe someone would be there.

The call rang once, twice.

"Pick up, pick up," he pleaded.

"Wolf Lake Consulting. LeVar Hopkins here."

He sat back and exhaled. "This is Elliot Saunders. Someone breached my network and erased my files, and the security monitors died."

A pause. "Mr. Saunders, are you alone?"

"Of course I'm alone. I'm trying to complete my work."

"Don't answer the door for anyone until I reach your house. I'll phone the sheriff's department while I drive."

The call ended. Saunders wanted to cry. He'd lost everything.

Though he kept backup files of his completed work, he assumed those were gone too. How could someone break into his cloud server and destroy everything he'd created?

The Wi-Fi. He hadn't unplugged the unit, which sat in his living room.

Saunders lunged for the door and froze. The knob was turning on its own.

~

LeVar's tires screeched as he stopped the black Chrysler Limited outside Saunders' home. The neighborhood appeared quiet, yet looks could be deceiving. While he crossed the lawn and rushed up the steps, he checked each window for a break-in but found nothing.

The door was unlocked. That wasn't good.

Entering a dark living room, he yelled. "Mr. Saunders, are you here?"

A thump came from deep within the home. LeVar removed his service weapon. He was no longer acting as a private investigator. This was police business.

"Saunders?"

"In the den."

He flipped a wall switch and lit the interior. Following the hallway to Saunders' voice, he located a closed door across from a bedroom.

"It's LeVar Hopkins."

The door opened. A haggard Saunders grabbed him by the shirt collar and pulled him inside before locking the door behind them.

"He's inside the house."

"The stalker?"

"I'm sure of it. He bypassed the security system, broke into my server, and deleted everything. All my work. All my files."

LeVar assessed the den, which contained more computer equipment and servers than he'd ever seen in a private residence. "You're safe now."

"Am I? It seems this guy can do anything he wants to me."

Saunders grabbed a security monitor and whipped it against the ground in disgust. The screen cracked.

"Destroying the equipment will solve nothing. Control yourself. The Nightshade County Sheriff's Department is on the way."

The words weren't out of LeVar's mouth when a cruiser pulled into the driveway. He recognized Lambert. LeVar ran back to the entrance and met him in the doorway.

"What do we have?" Lambert asked.

"This is Elliot Saunders' house. He's the guy who hired Wolf Lake Consulting."

"The one with the stalker?"

"Yeah."

Lambert entered the house. "Where is Saunders?"

"In the computer den. Look, he swears someone is inside, but I only found him."

"Think he's overreacting?"

"I doubt it. Someone hacked his security system and his computers."

They split up and checked the home, moving from room to room. LeVar took Saunders with him to ensure his safety. After the deputies investigated each room, they yelled, "Clear!"

While Lambert interviewed Saunders in the den, LeVar got to work. He turned on the surge protectors despite the AI programmer's protests. The security monitors started working again. Well, all but the one Saunders had destroyed.

The cameras gave LeVar a view of the yard, the areas outside the windows, and various rooms inside the home. The stalker had been here, but he was gone now.

Lambert returned to LeVar while Saunders sulked in a chair. "Stay with him. I want to check around the house and see what we're up against."

"I've got you covered."

Lambert exited the house while LeVar messaged Chelsey and Raven with the latest developments. Saunders was crying. How much had the man lost?

Though LeVar had checked every room in the house, he kept his service weapon ready. This stalker appeared capable of walking through walls, physical and digital. The screens showed Lambert kneeling in the backyard and shining a flashlight against the ground.

A few minutes later, Lambert returned and pulled LeVar into the hallway. He closed the door so Saunders couldn't overhear.

"Footprints in the backyard," Lambert said. "I couldn't find signs of a break-in, but my guess is the stalker didn't need to."

LeVar understood. "That's the issue with these digital door locks. If someone cracks the code, they can walk right inside. What do you want to do with Saunders?"

"He can't stay here tonight. I'll put in a call with the security firm and ensure they get someone out here ASAP. Right now, Saunders is a sitting duck."

The AI programmer didn't like the idea of staying with a friend overnight. From the way he balked, LeVar wondered if the man had any friends. In the end, Saunders complied. He would stay with a coworker in Harmon. Lambert would follow Saunders to the residence and keep him safe.

But the stalker was still out there. And LeVar knew he would come after Saunders again.

26

Inside the sheriff's department, Thomas set up a space heater and directed the warmth toward his deputies. The station's heating system was on the fritz again, and it was too late to call a repairperson.

"All we have to go on is a vague description of some guy no one recognized hanging around the sound system," Thomas said.

Aguilar didn't reply. She clenched her jaw and stared at the top of her desk, as if the answers lay in her reflection.

Emma sat a few desks away and huddled against the cold. If the county wouldn't pay to upgrade the facilities inside the sheriff's department, they would have to move. Either that or keep suffering whenever the heating and cooling system failed.

"Any ideas?" he asked.

Aguilar opened her desk drawer, checked for an object she apparently couldn't locate, and slammed it shut. "We interviewed a few dozen people who attended the vigil. I suggest we turn our focus back to the list of convicts. This time, let's concentrate on anyone released during the last year."

She had a point. The distorted voice that had disrupted

Emma's speech made Thomas believe Hannah's killer was back. He couldn't imagine someone playing a sick joke just to shock everyone.

"He said Hannah's name," Emma pointed out without looking at them.

Aguilar wasn't so sure. "Are we positive? I couldn't tell what the man said."

"Play the video again," Thomas said.

They'd recorded the vigil to catch the killer if he showed his face. But now all they had was a mishmash of people crowding the stage and sudden panic when the killer's voice claimed control. Thomas pulled up a chair as Aguilar set the video's timestamp to just before the incident. Emma turned her head, as if she couldn't bear hearing the man again.

Through the tinny computer speakers, a screech of feedback marked the saboteur beginning to talk. Thomas placed his face close to the screen and listened. Distortion made it impossible to determine what the man said, but he believed Hannah's name came through the audio system.

"There it is," the sheriff said. "He's saying something about Hannah's kidnapping."

"I can't tell," Aguilar said, unwilling to commit.

From the haunted expression on Emma's face, it was clear she agreed with Thomas.

"Play it again."

Aguilar did as Thomas requested. The voice came through, and this time the lead deputy bobbed her head. "You might be right. That sounded like 'Hannah,' but I can't hear the rest. Is he boasting that he took her?"

"I think so." Thomas glanced at Emma for a reaction. The journalist left her chair and paced by the windows. "All right, take the recording back to the beginning. I want every male cataloged. Flag anyone you don't recognize."

"Right away, Thomas."

They had to catch this guy before he struck again. Thomas remembered Tiffany and the two boys who'd sneaked inside the abandoned home down the road from the elementary and middle schools. He and Lambert had found food wrappers and confirmed someone was using the so-called haunted house. But was the intruder a person who needed a place to live? Or was their killer spying on children through the windows?

Patrol units had failed to catch anyone using the house since the night they'd investigated. It was conceivable the killer had snatched Hannah off the sidewalk and taken her inside the home, concealing the girl until dark. Then what? Had he dumped the body where nobody would find it?

"Here's a guy I don't recognize," Aguilar said. She zoomed in on the man, drew a box around his face, and captured a still image. "And this person. He's not from Wolf Lake."

"Good work. I want every face cross-referenced with the list of recently released convicts."

"You're assuming our unsub did time. Maybe he was free all along."

Thomas had to consider the possibility. The implications chilled him: What if their killer had remained active, traveling from one state to the next to throw off the authorities? And now he was back.

A message arrived from Lambert. The deputy had accompanied Elliot Saunders to a friend's house in Harmon. Now the Saunders stalking case was a police matter.

"The second Lambert returns from Harmon," Thomas said, "bring him up to speed on the people you couldn't identify in the video."

"I'll need his help."

"Definitely." He searched for Emma and spotted her near the entrance. As had been the case when the journalist went for a walk by herself, his unease grew. "Emma, stay away from the doors."

She returned to the rows of desks and sat. "Do you think this guy is watching me?"

"Possibly. Better safe than sorry." He narrowed his eyes and tapped a pen against his leg. "Emma, are you still staying at that hotel between Treman Mills and Wolf Lake?"

"The Bernhardt Resort, yes."

"Not anymore. After tonight, I can't allow you to stay alone."

The journalist lifted her chin. "I'm not afraid of this guy."

"You should be, and I don't want another tragedy on my hands."

Aguilar turned away from the computer screen. "I agree with the sheriff. This guy spoke Hannah's name during your speech. That tells me he's targeting you."

"Emma, have you noticed anyone hanging around the resort who looked like they didn't belong?"

The journalist thought for a long moment. "Not that I recall."

"What about people trailing you on the road?"

"No, sir."

The killer was following her. He was careful enough so she didn't see.

"What are you thinking, Thomas?" Aguilar asked.

"Emma, I want you to stay with me." He saw the discomfort on her face and hurried to explain. "With me and my fiancée. Chelsey heads up Wolf Lake Consulting with her partner, Raven Hopkins. That means two people can watch your back and keep you safe."

"Are you sure this is necessary?" Emma asked. "I don't want to impose."

"I won't sleep a wink if I know you're alone out at Bernhardt's. Even a hotel in the center of Wolf Lake won't do. You're not safe until we take this creep off the streets."

"But I'm intruding."

"Nonsense. We have a guest room on the top floor. The house sits on Wolf Lake, and one of my junior deputies rents the guest house. Between me, Chelsey, and LeVar, we'll have three trained investigators to watch over you."

Emma bit her nails. "If you insist, I guess I can stay at your place. But the second my presence makes you uncomfortable—"

"It won't." He nodded at Aguilar. "Have a deputy follow Emma back to the hotel so she can gather her belongings."

"Will do," Aguilar said.

This could work. With Thomas and Chelsey in the house and LeVar out back, Emma would be safe from the killer. Aguilar pulled a deputy aside and briefed him on the situation. The other officer glanced at Emma, then clamped on his shoulder holster.

"I have one important question," Thomas said to Emma. "Are you allergic to animals?"

Emma scrunched her forehead in confusion. "No. Why?"

"That's a relief. Do you like dogs?"

"Sure, I love dogs."

"All right then. Wait until you get a load of Jack."

"Who is Jack?"

Thomas grinned. "You'll see. He's harmless, but I wouldn't leave out any articles where he can eat them."

The commandeered deputy arrived at the desk where Emma sat. After a quick introduction, he escorted the journalist through the doors and to the parking lot.

As they climbed into a cruiser, Thomas surveyed the empty road outside the office. One driver at the end of the block turned off their headlights. Probably someone returning home and nothing to worry about. Even so, Thomas watched until the person exited their vehicle, climbed the steps to a Cape Cod house, and twisted the key into the lock.

False alarm.

But Thomas was sure the killer was in Wolf Lake. Waiting for Emma to make the wrong move.

Then he would take her, as he had Hannah.

27

Though Thomas had only slept three hours last night, he'd done so without worry. With Emma tucked inside the guest room and his and Chelsey's bedroom between the stairs and the journalist, he knew she was protected.

How did Chelsey feel about an attractive woman staying with them? They were supposed to write more invitations and plan the wedding, and here he was inviting Emma into their home. For her part, Chelsey hadn't balked. Not that Thomas had expected she would. His future wife would go to any length to protect someone in need. Still, he felt a little guilty for bringing a woman into the house.

This morning, Emma was meeting another member of the family—Scout Mourning. When he'd explained that the teenager was a technology guru and could help narrow the search for Hannah's killer, Emma looked confused. Right now, they were working together at the dining room table where he'd last seen them. Chelsey would follow Emma to the sheriff's department afterward, then start her day at Wolf Lake Consulting.

He mussed his hair—Mother always referred to it as an unruly mop—and watched one of Nolan Trevino's videos. Aguilar had located a sketchy-looking VHS machine in the supply room, and after blowing a generation of dust off the player, they'd hooked it up to his computer. As he watched the footage, the computer captured the images and saved them on the hard drive. Now he had a digital version of the videotape.

On the screen, four children—one boy and three girls of indeterminate ages—climbed up the steps to the fort in the village park. He guessed they were somewhere between eight and eleven, but it was impossible to tell unless Nolan zoomed in. The camera operator swung the lens toward a group of trees, where a vulture flew across the sky. Then the picture displayed colorful wildflowers growing in the grass.

The bobbing, shifting view gave Thomas motion sickness. He paused the recording and waited for his equilibrium to return.

Who was he kidding? Nolan Trevino was harmless, and there was nothing incriminating on these videotapes. Plus, Nolan was dead, and the killer was still at large. This was a waste of time. Had so many Wolf Lake residents not blamed the poor man for the disappearing children, the sheriff wouldn't have spent another second studying the recordings.

He thought of Nolan's family. The sister wanted him to clear the man's name. And he would. But not today.

Maggie's voice carried from the entryway as Chelsey dropped off Emma. Before Thomas could emerge from his office to say hello, his fiancée rushed to her car and drove toward the private investigations firm. Tonight, he would help with the invitations. He owed her.

Emma was briefing a very interested Lambert about her night in the guest room. Tigger had made an appearance, and Jack had slept at the foot of the bed, as if the dog sensed it was his duty to protect her from a killer. She'd slept well, then rose and helped Chelsey feed the pets before Scout arrived. All this time, Jack had trailed Emma from room to room, never letting her out of his sight until she showered. Even then, the dog was waiting outside the bathroom.

"Sounds like an eventful night," Lambert said.

"Not so much." Emma caught Thomas's eye when he walked out of his office. "I appreciate everyone's kindness. I can't recall the last time so many people looked out for my best interest."

A lump formed in Thomas's throat. This woman had overcome so much.

"Did you get any work done?" Thomas asked. "Or did Jack consume all your time?"

Emma set her laptop on an open desk. "I accomplished a ton. And thanks to your neighbor Scout, I think we had a breakthrough this morning."

"On the kidnapping case?"

"Yes. Take a gander at this." She turned on the computer and loaded a digital document that contained forum posts. "I believe the man who abducted Hannah and the other girls wrote these messages."

Lambert moved closer to the screen. "Where did you find these posts?"

"On community forums and news websites. Remember, social media hadn't been a thing when Hannah vanished. Back then, people used these websites to share opinions and discuss current events. It's no surprise that the kidnappings drew so much attention."

"I'm amazed the forums are still online," Thomas said, sitting beside Emma.

"Some aren't. We used the Wayback Machine to find a few. Don't criminals interject themselves into investigations?"

"Yes," Lambert said, "but they do it for different reasons.

Some believe they can influence the police by planting false information."

"To make the trail go cold?"

"Right. Others are so obsessed that they need to discuss the crimes with anyone who will listen. They often appear helpful, as if they're trying to solve the investigation. But obviously they aren't."

Thomas asked, "How did you zero in on these conversations? They must be fifteen to twenty-five years old."

"I theorized the kidnapper would become most active during the time of the abductions. But there was no way I could read every message. That's where Scout came in. She used software to identify similar writing styles."

"Ah, right. Scout is doing the same for Wolf Lake Consulting to help catch a stalker."

"We found four potential suspects. All these people hid behind screen names and posted after a kidnapping occurred. Check the dates of the abductions. There is a spike in activity on several forums after each child disappeared."

"That could be community outrage."

"Without a doubt, but I think there's more to these messages than rage. Every person we identified seemed to know a little too much about the kidnappings. Unless the police and media were feeding them information, they had first-hand knowledge."

Thomas was impressed. "This is terrific. These screen names give us something to go on. Was Scout able to pull their IP addresses?"

"No, but she's running more searches for recent forum and social media posts. Once the software spots similar writing styles, she'll send you the list."

This was a tremendous breakthrough. The killer had to slip up at some point and give revealing information. Thomas wondered if he'd been wrong to search for incarcerated criminals that matched the profile. Maybe the killer had been loose all this time.

"We're on the verge of catching this guy," Thomas said. At that moment, Aguilar entered the station to start her shift. "Aguilar, Lambert, I want both of you to work with Emma. I'm not totally abandoning the criminal database yet, so ensure everyone we shortlisted was out of prison when these messages were written. And I want all three of you to check online for people discussing last night's vigil. If Emma's theory is correct, our unsub took part in the discussion."

Aguilar tossed her jacket over a chair and joined Lambert.

Thomas hoped this was the breakthrough they needed to solve the case. He grabbed a mug of green tea from the breakroom and returned to his office. A mountain of videotapes stared him in the face. He took a sip and drummed his fingers on the desk. Nolan Trevino was harmless, yet the footage drew Thomas like a fly to honey. What was it about these recordings that pulled him?

Maggie alerted the sheriff to an incoming call. He pressed the blinking light on his desk.

"Sheriff Shepherd here."

"Sheriff, this is Roger Crankshaw at the Behavioral Analysis Unit. You got a minute?"

"Fire away."

"I've been going over the details of your child abduction cases. This is highly unusual, as the unsub was active for well over a decade before falling off the grid."

"That's what I thought," Thomas said, picking up a pen to record anything Crankshaw had to say.

"There isn't a ton to go on, but I constructed a profile for you. I'll send the report to your email, but let me give you a condensed version now."

"Ready when you are."

Crankshaw took a breath. "The individual in question is a white male, age thirty to forty-five years. This age range is indicative of an unsub with both the means and opportunity to plan and execute abductions with a degree of premeditation. The abductor exhibits a need to exert control and dominion over others, likely stemming from feelings of powerlessness or inadequacy in other areas of his life. This control is not just physical but also psychological, as he seeks to manipulate and dominate the will of his victims."

"What about his personal life?"

"He's likely to be a loner or socially isolated individual who struggles with meaningful adult relationships. This isolation could be self-imposed or a result of social rejection. His interactions with adults, especially peers, are uncomfortable. The individual spends a considerable amount of time in fantasy, where he imagines scenarios involving control and domination. These fantasies are a crucial part of the motivation for his crimes, serving as both rehearsal and escalation of his desires."

"Where would he carry out these fantasies?"

"He'd need privacy. His home, but that's risky."

"What about an abandoned property?" asked Thomas.

"Now you're talking."

"Okay, tell me more about this guy. What does his behavior stem from?"

"He shows a specific preference for female children within a narrow age range, indicating a fixed sexual interest in prepubescent victims. This preference is part of what drives his selection process. The unsub may view victims as possessions or trophies. This behavior underscores his objectification of the victims and detachment from their humanity."

Thomas scribbled the information. "Why haven't we caught him?"

"He's skilled. The unsub likely uses manipulation or deceit

to gain a victim's trust before abduction, possibly posing as an authority figure or fabricating scenarios that require the child's assistance. He may have a history of antisocial behavior or criminal activities, including but not limited to acts of violence, property crimes, or sexual offenses. It's possible the individual experienced neglect, abuse, or trauma in his childhood, which has contributed to his development of harmful behaviors and attitudes. I'll have more in the full report."

"This is terrific, Agent Crankshaw."

"My pleasure. And Sheriff?"

"Yes, sir?"

"Take this guy off the street."

After the call ended, Thomas pushed another tape into the VHS player. Static covered the screen, and a crunching noise came from the machine. The player was eating the tape.

Before Thomas lost the footage, he stopped the machine and carefully pried open the door. A maze of black tape wrapped around the heads. Pulling the recording from the machine would tear it apart. Was it a big deal? There were more recordings sitting on his desk.

Yes, this was important, though he didn't know why. He could be obsessive-compulsive. His parents had told him as much when he was young, and he was still prone to these behaviors.

He followed his instincts. From his desk drawer, he removed a screwdriver and went to work. If he had to take apart the VHS player, he would save that recording.

28

Emma set the walkie-talkie on the passenger's seat. Thomas had given her the device so she could keep in contact with him and the deputies. The two-way radio gave her a measure of comfort as she drove through the dark from the station to the sheriff's home on Wolf Lake.

Illuminated by the headlights, mile markers shot out of the night and appeared to lurch off the shoulder. She was tired and anxious. That was expected after twelve hours searching for a kidnapper.

The journalist yawned and turned down the radio, which squawked with static. She kept it just loud enough that she would hear someone attempting to reach her. In the mirror, a bread truck tailed her by a few car lengths before it swerved onto the highway.

Had it not been dark, she could have seen the hill that overlooked her old neighborhood, where life as she'd known it had stopped. And if she could see that rise, maybe she might glimpse the street where she'd grown up, the sidewalk that led from the school to her home, or the turn she might have taken when Hannah broke off and walked to the store.

Emma wiped a tear from her eye. Her old friend seemed to call from the night, begging her to right the wrong that had stolen her from this world. She would. With Thomas Shepherd's aid, she would catch the kidnapper and make sure he paid for his crimes. The sheriff was a respectable man, someone who wouldn't stop until they located the person who'd taken those girls.

A text arrived. She gave the screen a quick glance as she drove. That wasn't a smart idea, but she kept the car in its lane. The message said something about Chelsey running late and the house being empty. Thomas's future wife wouldn't arrive home for another fifteen minutes.

Emma appreciated everyone looking out for her, but she'd stayed alone in a hotel room until yesterday. Were the kidnapper searching for her, he could have struck at any time. Yet he hadn't, and that told her it was pointless to worry. She had the walkie-talkie, her phone, and a wolflike dog named Jack awaiting her arrival. There was no reason to believe she was in danger.

When the high beams lit the mirror, she squinted and checked behind. A vehicle followed, though she couldn't see past the headlights. It was probably someone who wanted to get home and hadn't realized his brights were on. She adjusted the mirror so the reflection didn't blind her and drove on.

She started down the lake road. Another two miles, and she'd arrive at the lakeside A-frame.

But the vehicle was closer now. Almost bumper to bumper.

"Go around," she said, as if the man could hear.

The driver fell back and gave her room, but he was still there. How long had the vehicle followed? By her estimation, at least two miles.

With one hand on the wheel, she reached for the walkie-talkie. She wasn't sure what to say. There was a driver on the same road as her, but that was about it. The deputies would think she was losing her mind.

Another glance at the mirror. Still there. Closer.

Emma pressed the accelerator, and the car shot forward. She waited for the tailgater to speed up, but he gave her space.

"Stop panicking," she whispered as she drove. "People live on this road, and I was driving too slow."

The person behind her wasn't a madman, just an irritated driver searching for the right time to pass. Ahead of her, the double line broke into a passing lane. A yellow sign along the road advised passers to use caution. This was his chance to get around her car.

One hand on the radio, the other on the wheel. Eyes darting between the road ahead and the mirror. She was asking for a wreck.

Without turning on his blinker, the trailing driver turned left and disappeared down a dark lane. She exhaled and set down the walkie-talkie.

Now that the false danger had passed, she spotted Thomas's house and turned into the driveway. The downstairs lights were on, as was the porch light, making it easy for her to see.

As she crossed the lawn, her shoes squishing against the soggy terrain, a monstrous shape leaped up and pressed against the window. Her heart stopped.

It was Jack. The dog wore a grin of recognition. When she stuck her key into the lock, he was right there. Jack greeted her with a slobbery lick across the face. She giggled and coaxed him to sit. She looked over her shoulder and confirmed nobody had followed her to the sheriff's house.

Safe. And Chelsey would arrive in minutes.

Wanting to make herself useful, she said, "Hey, boy. Can I feed you and your little brother?"

Tigger crept out from behind the couch and rubbed against her shin, purring.

In the refrigerator, she located their homemade meals. Thomas and Chelsey had stopped feeding the pets store-bought kibble, opting instead for healthy food. Jack gulped down his portion in seconds while Tigger took a dainty bite. As the cat ate, she turned to the dog.

"Ready to go outside?"

Jack wagged his tail. Beyond the glass door, the night was pitch-black, but she felt safe. No one in their right mind would attack her with the enormous dog on guard.

The dog squatted beside a tree. She scanned the lake, which sloshed against the shoreline. Nobody was home at LeVar's house, but lights shone inside the Mournings' property. Her head swiveled back and forth, eyes interrogating the shadows.

"Hurry, boy. It's chilly out here."

~

HE STOPPED the car down the road from Sheriff Shepherd's house. A light turned on outside, and he saw her.

The girl who'd gotten away.

Their lives had come full circle, hadn't they? As the years passed, he'd never forgotten her. Now she worked as a reporter and investigated Hannah's disappearance.

If only Emma realized he'd wanted *her* all along, that he'd settled for Hannah because she walked past the abandoned house down the road from the two schools. Inside, he'd found it easy to observe girls passing by. Even today, he used the house whenever he wanted to.

And the need was back. Stronger than ever. She'd grown too old to fit his type, but he would take her. Too many decades had escaped him before the urge returned to take Emma Walsh. If only she knew his interest had been rekindled by her articles.

About him. How ironic.

He'd almost snatched her coming out the hotel, but the timing had been wrong. The sun hadn't set, and a hotel clerk had been smoking in the parking lot.

The man climbed out of his car and approached the A-frame. He lived in Wolf Lake again, and he could afford to be patient.

But he wanted her. Now.

Looking out for traffic and not wanting anyone to spot him, he crossed the lake road. He could smell the water from here. The lake emitted the scents of melted ice and something that reminded him of ozone.

This was the time. With the sheriff and the private investigator gone, he would take Emma. Smirking, he approached the yard.

And stopped when he saw the hulking figure on four legs. That damned dog. Had it not been for the mutt, he would have sliced all their throats while they slept last night.

Then the dog swerved in his direction. Even from the next yard, he saw the fur standing on its back. A growl made him retreat a step.

Emma grabbed the dog by the collar and coaxed him inside. Stupid woman. The dog would have taken him out and saved her life.

The man didn't mind waiting. He knew where she was staying.

His time would come.

29

Thomas turned on the stove and waited for the oil in the pan to heat. He'd awakened early, hoping to make breakfast for Chelsey and Emma before they started their day. Outside the window, spring sunshine lit the water and threw golden hues against the guesthouse, where LeVar appeared to be vacuuming.

The clock read six. He cracked the eggs and stepped back when the sizzling oil leaped out of the pan. Turning down the heat, he pushed the eggs around with a spatula and hummed to himself. If this was a preview of his future life, he couldn't wait to sign up. Just Thomas and Chelsey, plus two pets who kept them entertained. These were simple joys, but he cherished them.

Footsteps moving across the ceiling told him the women were awake. Seconds later, Jack raced down the stairs and sat by his side, watching him cook with great interest. Tigger would follow when he was ready. There was no rushing the tabby.

"Morning," Chelsey said, planting a kiss on his cheek. Her mussed hair made her even more alluring, if possible. "You didn't have to cook breakfast."

"I enjoy the work."

"I can tell."

She appeared ready to kiss him on the lips before Emma padded into the kitchen.

"Hold that thought," he said, and Chelsey winked.

"Ready for another day?" Thomas asked the journalist. "I have a good feeling about today."

"Think we'll catch him?" Emma asked.

"I do. Between the research you and Scout did and the faces we pulled from the cameras overlooking the vigil, we're bound to catch a break."

"Can I help you cook?"

"I have everything under control. Sit with Chelsey. Breakfast will be ready soon."

At the dining room table, the women sat across from each other. He admired Chelsey for putting the wedding plans on hold and allowing the beautiful reporter to share their home. They barely knew one another, but Chelsey and Emma carried on as if they were long-lost friends.

"This must be so difficult for you," Chelsey said from the next room.

Emma didn't answer. She lowered her head and studied the tabletop. The poor woman seemed wracked with guilt. Why did she blame herself for Hannah's kidnapping? Emma had been in no position to stop a killer at twelve.

Thomas plated the food and passed dishes around the table. He sat beside Chelsey and unfolded a napkin in his lap, as if he were eating at a restaurant. Father had taught him to be respectful when he was young, and he never grew out of the habit, no matter where he ate his meals. He sometimes caught himself placing a napkin on his thighs when he was alone in the house.

"Emma and Scout have been a great help with the kidnapping investigation," Thomas said between bites.

"I wish Wolf Lake Consulting could offer more assistance," said Chelsey, "but we're busy with the Elliot Saunders case, especially now that the stalker broke into his home."

Emma looked from Thomas to Chelsey. "Elliot Saunders? As in the artificial intelligence guru?"

"Do you know him?"

"I wrote an article about Saunders several months ago. Interesting guy. He's as talented as they come, but he's not so good with people."

Chelsey clasped her hands. "What do you mean?"

"He steps on others to get ahead. I've seen it before—hyper-aggressive technology types who think the only way forward is through the person standing in their way."

"Doesn't sound like you think much of him."

"He's the local leader in a very competitive business," Emma said. "I'm in no position to question his methods."

As Emma took another bite, Chelsey leaned forward. "Emma, can you give me the names of people Saunders stepped on?"

"There's your motive," Thomas said, sawing a piece of bacon with his fork.

"It adds up, but Saunders swears he gets along with his associates."

"He does," said Emma, "until they become larger than him."

Chelsey grabbed Thomas's notepad from the table and tore off a sheet. "After breakfast, can you give me a list? I'm looking for anyone who threatened to overtake Saunders."

"The associates I interviewed were at least a few steps below Elliot Saunders, but I'll go through my notes and see what I can find."

~

At nine o'clock, LeVar put the finishing touches on a vegan breakfast sandwich from The Broken Yolk. He rubbed his stomach, which wasn't flabby like Raven swore it would become, and tossed the paper bag into the recycling bin.

"Not bad," his sister said from the next desk. "That's two breakfast sandwiches already, and you knocked off three donuts before I arrived. You really need to watch what you eat and how much you consume."

"It's healthy, yo."

"Since when are donuts healthy?"

"They aren't, but the vegan sandwiches balance everything out."

"Do they, now?"

"Hundred percent."

Across the room, Chelsey rolled her eyes. Scout was at school today, and though LeVar relied on the girl's technological prowess, he felt relieved. Yesterday, she'd worn a skirt and sat knee-to-knee with him. He refused to look at her as more than a friend, though fate kept placing them in these positions.

"You look troubled," Raven said.

"Nah. I'm thinking about my exam schedule. Gotta ace my finals in May."

"Didn't Kane Grove accept you?"

"Yeah, but there's more scholarship money for A-students than there are for reformed gangsters who pull B's." He rolled up the sleeves on his sweatshirt and rubbed his hands together. "Now that we have those names Emma Walsh gave to Chelsey, we can look into each and determine who our stalker is."

"If he's on the list," Chelsey said. "Emma stressed that she spoke to low-level members of Saunders' team. The higher-ups wouldn't talk, and nobody wanted to out their leader and risk retaliation."

"I told you this guy made enemies. All this time, we've looked at technophobes. This stalker is someone Saunders ticked off."

"Saunders isn't the nice guy he pretends to be," said Raven, "but he's still our client. We have to serve his interests, and right now that means keeping him safe."

"The stalker dude busted through his network defenses like they weren't there. Our suspect has mad skills."

"As strong as Saunders?" Chelsey asked.

"To bypass his security system, delete his files, and escape the house before I arrived, I'd have to say he's excellent at what he does. And that scares me. We can't watch Saunders 24-7."

"We have to try," Raven said, tossing a packet on his desk. "This is our client's dossier. It includes everything he's accomplished, the people he worked with, and his schedule for the next week."

LeVar lifted the schedule and whistled. "A conference in Syracuse today, a speaking engagement at Harmon High School tomorrow morning, followed by an in-studio interview at a Rochester television station during the afternoon. And this is only over the next two days."

"He's always on the move," Chelsey said. "That gives our suspect countless opportunities to attack. How free are you through tomorrow?"

"You saw the schedule the AI program produced. I can help after my afternoon class lets out today. Tomorrow, I'm free after eleven."

"What about your deputy duties?"

"Not an issue," LeVar said. "Thomas only has me working Sunday afternoon."

"Raven, you're our personal security expert. Can you put

together a plan that lets us watch Saunders through tomorrow afternoon?"

Raven tossed her hair. "I'll get right to it."

"Thank you. Saunders is staying at his friend's house again tonight. LeVar, can you trail him until he arrives?"

"No problem."

"All right, team. Our client is at his office. I'll drive over and follow him to Syracuse. If we're lucky, the stalker will show his face."

"You really want that, Chelsey?" Raven asked.

"I'm just waiting for him to make a mistake."

30

Every time a crackling, crunching noise came out of the VHS player, Thomas cringed. Nolan Trevino's videotapes weren't in the best shape, but neither was the machine. These recordings held vital information. Thomas couldn't afford to let the player shred the recording.

"What's that sound?" Aguilar asked, poking her head into his office.

"The videotapes."

"That sounds bad, Thomas."

He massaged his forehead. "I'm aware. Listen, we don't have a head cleaner in the supply room, do we?"

She screwed up her face. "A head cleaner? Oh, I know what you mean. Talk about a blast from the past. Remember when we had to clean the machines, or they would devour our recordings?"

"Unfortunately, I do. I'm afraid that if I don't intervene, the player will eat Nolan Trevino's videos. Do shops still sell cleaners?"

Aguilar shrugged. "If they do, I've never seen one. I bet you can find them in those big box electronic stores."

"Hmm. The closest one is at the Syracuse mall."

"Are these tapes really that important?"

He rolled his chair out from behind the desk and stretched his legs. "They are. Nolan isn't a killer, and I want to prove it."

"But we have all those names from the message boards and prison databases to sift through. Is this the best use of our time?"

"I have a hunch, Aguilar."

She grinned. "Whenever you get a hunch, we catch a killer."

"I sure hope that's the case this time."

After she returned to her work, he started the recording. The tape was behaving. For now. As the images played out on the screen, the computer captured them in digital format so he wouldn't lose anything.

The view bounced from a group of teenagers riding bikes to a butterfly lighting on a flower. If Thomas were there to see these images in person, he'd consider them wonderful. But he was dizzy again. He popped an anti-motion sickness pill into his mouth and hoped it wouldn't leave him too groggy to work.

Back and forth, the camera tracked a world to which Nolan desperately wanted to belong. Nobody had played with the autistic man when he was a boy, and Thomas understood how he felt. Thomas had experienced similar ostracizing at school, but he was fortunate to have a few friends in the neighborhood who had looked past his Asperger's.

He couldn't blame kids for not appreciating differences. The frontal cortex of the brain didn't fully develop until the age of twenty-five. How could anyone expect children to figure things out by themselves? This was on the parents; they needed to teach their kids right from wrong and why including children different from them was the correct thing to do.

On the screen, the view lifted skyward and fell back to the earth. The jostling motion told Thomas that Nolan was on the move. His eyes crossed, and his stomach turned.

"Stand still for a while," he muttered at the screen.

One pill wouldn't save him from another dizzy spell. He grabbed the packet and considered taking a second, but the directions stated only one every six hours.

Thomas thought about taking a break. The other deputies needed his help to work through all those names, and he agreed with Aguilar that the list took priority.

"That's enough for now, Nolan."

But when he reached for the remote control, the camera focused on a figure across the park. It was a man, and he wasn't sitting on a bench and watching over the children like a parent would. Instead, he stood behind a row of trees, as if spying on the kids.

What were the odds that Nolan had caught Hannah Clarke's kidnapper on video? Steep. This had to be someone else, perhaps a maintenance worker or some adult taking a walk.

Except this man didn't seem interested in exercise. He stood among the shadows and stared toward the swing set, where a girl kicked her legs out as the swing descended in an arc. How old was she? The girl was too far away to know for sure, but Thomas guessed she was about ten. The age fit the killer's type.

The camera swung away for a second, and when it returned to the tree line, the man was gone.

Thomas sat forward and rubbed his eyes. Was he jumping to conclusions? The man in the park could have been anyone.

A second later, the tape crunched again. He stopped the player and ripped the recording from the machine before he lost it. Assessing the damage, he concluded that this videotape was the worst of the bunch.

"Boss man?"

Thomas jumped out of his skin. He hadn't seen Lambert in the doorway.

"Sorry for scaring you. The team is getting the munchies. As it's almost noon, I could grab food and bring it back to the station."

"Lunch sounds great right now."

"Outstanding. Emma wants to go. Do you mind if I follow her to the deli?"

"What do you have in mind, Lambert?"

The deputy looked back at Emma, who was donning a coat. "I thought about what you said—that the kidnapper might be back. What if we made it seem like she was on her own? I could hang back and observe her movements."

"This seems risky."

"Thomas, I won't let her out of my sight."

What if the kidnapper snatched Emma before Lambert arrived to help?

That was nonsensical. His deputy wouldn't allow harm to befall the woman.

"I'm willing to agree," Thomas said, "but I want you right behind at all times."

"Got that."

~

THE MAN HID inside a car parked two blocks from the station. With a pair of binoculars, he could see Emma through the windows. He only lifted the binoculars now and then. He didn't want to attract unwanted attention.

Too bad he couldn't snatch her yet. Not with so many cops around.

He started the car, intent on changing position, when the journalist shrugged into a jacket and exited the station.

Was this really happening? She was by herself.

He scanned the street. Few people crowded the sidewalks. Though it was daytime, he believed he could grab Emma and toss her into his car before someone spotted him. Hell, he'd done the same thing countless times with children.

The engine rumbled. He rolled off the curb and followed the woman, who was heading into the village center, where the eateries were. The crowd would grow there. He couldn't let her get that far.

Pulling onto the empty roadway, he coasted behind her. Wary of a trap, he searched for a deputy but found no one.

Before Emma reached the village center, she entered a deli on Fourth Street. He cursed.

An idea occurred to him. What if he walked into the deli and ordered lunch? He could walk right up to her, and she wouldn't suspect anything.

But as he neared the deli, an imposing deputy with a buzz cut materialized on the sidewalk. It was as if the officer had teleported from the station.

The man swung the car to the curb and parked behind a flower delivery van. He shut off the engine and looked for somewhere to hide. The deputy was coming.

Running would cause suspicion. He waited as the deputy's shadow grew closer. With nowhere to go, he slipped beneath the wheel and crouched between the seat and dashboard. Footsteps scuffed the pavement. He sensed the deputy right outside the car. Probably staring through the window.

But when he lifted his head and peeked, the deputy had continued down the sidewalk on patrol.

So this was how it was. The officers knew he was after Emma.

No matter. If he had to kill everyone who stood between him and the girl who got away, he would.

31

LeVar bit the corner of a peanut butter and jelly sandwich and wiped the crumbs from his mouth. After class, he'd driven straight to Syracuse, where Elliot Saunders was giving a speech on the future of AI technology in the classroom.

He checked the time and glanced around the lecture hall. From the back of the room, he observed the attendees. Most were Caucasian males, some balding. Everyone listened with rapt attention as Saunders spoke.

Nobody looked suspicious or had approached the stage. So far, so good.

It was LeVar's job to monitor Saunders during the conference, then follow him to Harmon, where he would work in his office until nine. Did the AI guru never sleep?

A message arrived from Raven. She wanted him to call her. LeVar stepped out of the lecture hall and closed the door.

"What's up?"

"We're working through the names on Emma Walsh's list," Raven said. "Chelsey and I found one interesting suspect."

He shifted the phone to his opposite ear and removed a notepad from his jacket. "Talk to me."

"A guy named Ian Mercer. He worked with Saunders for two years. This was prior to Saunders releasing his technology."

"What's so special about Mercer?"

"Saunders fired him. I found no explanation for the dismissal, and I can't imagine why anyone would get rid of Mercer."

"Intelligent?"

Raven chuckled. "You don't know the half. Ian Mercer earned a Master of Science in Artificial Intelligence from Carnegie Mellon. He picked up a Ph.D. in Computer Science from the same institution."

LeVar whistled. "He's a real smarty pants."

"That's one way to put it."

"Okay, Mercer is a guy you want to build a company around, especially when you're developing cutting edge technology. That tells me Saunders and Mercer had personal differences, which made it impossible for them to work together. Or Mercer was growing faster than the firm."

"Both are plausible assumptions."

"Which fits my theory that our stalker is jealous of Saunders, not afraid of AI. It could be Mercer. What more do we know about this guy?"

"He lives in Fayetteville, which is outside of Syracuse," said Raven.

"That means he's close enough to follow Saunders from place to place and break into his house. Do you have a photograph?"

"Hold up." Raven typed in the background. "You should have it now."

A picture appeared on his screen. Unlike the nerdy cliches hanging out inside the lecture room, Ian Mercer was a physical specimen. Rounded biceps. Light-brown hair. In many circles, women would have found him attractive. There was something about the man's eyes that LeVar didn't trust. As if he saw into your soul whenever he looked at you.

"Thanks."

"I'll send you an article from a technology website about their falling out. The dismissal garnered attention."

"What should I do?"

"Keep watching Saunders and check the crowd for Mercer. I'm not saying he's our stalker, but he fits your profile. Just use discretion. I don't want Mercer to know we're onto him."

"You don't have to tell me. This isn't my first rodeo."

"Well, then, LeVar. Ride 'em, cowboy."

He ended the call and looked around the lobby. Several attendees sipped coffee and mingled outside the hall. One man threw his hands up in animation, obviously disagreeing with Saunders' assertions. Ian Mercer wasn't among them.

LeVar reentered the room and waited for his eyes to adjust to the darkness. When he could see, he returned to his seat at the back, where he initiated a thorough search of each row. After assessing the many faces and too many balding heads, he settled on three people who could have been Ian Mercer. It was impossible to tell. The lighting conditions were abysmal.

"You're here, aren't you?" LeVar whispered.

A woman turned in disapproval and shushed him. He mouthed an apology.

The speech continued. Side-stage, someone straightened a microphone cord.

Saunders concluded his presentation without warning. Before LeVar realized what was happening, a throng of attendees filled the aisles and pushed toward the exits. Was Mercer in the crowd?

He climbed over a seat and reached the next row as people

marched past. No sign of Mercer. Still, LeVar sensed the stalker was here.

With one eye on Saunders, who snapped a briefcase shut on the stage, and another on the exiting lecture guests, LeVar was trying to catch two rabbits at once. As expected, he lost both.

The last of the attendees filed out of the hall, leaving an empty stage. Where was Saunders?

LeVar remembered the person hidden offstage. He sprinted down the aisle and hopped up, almost toppling the podium.

"Saunders? Where are you?"

No reply.

He squeezed between two college-age women who'd come out to remove the podium. They gave him curious glances as he hurried past.

Spinning back to them, he asked, "Have either of you seen Elliot Saunders?"

The first woman shook her head, but the second pointed at a side door.

"He was carrying his supplies into the parking lot," she said.

Stupid man. Saunders was supposed to remain in sight. How could LeVar protect him if he ran off?

The off-duty deputy burst into the daylight and shielded his forehead. The sun was so bright, it burned his vision. Through watery eyes, he searched the parking lot until he spotted a lanky man in blue jeans and a trendy jacket loading a briefcase into his car.

Elliot Saunders.

LeVar was out of breath when he reached the man. "What in the hell were you thinking?"

Saunders looked down his nose at him. "Excuse me?"

"Leaving the lecture hall without waiting for me. You want me to protect you, right?"

"Please, Mr. Hopkins. I was only loading my car. The parking lot is full of people, and I had no intention of leaving without you."

"Don't do it again."

Saunders raised his hands in placation. "My apologies. I promise to follow your lead from now on. Did you see any suspicious activity during my speech?"

"It was hella-dark in there. I did my best."

"That's all I ask," Saunders said, opening the driver's side door. "I take it you'll follow me to Harmon? If I don't reconstruct the code the stalker stole, I'll lose my business."

"Tell me about Ian Mercer."

The AI guru stopped. "What about him?"

"You fired Mercer four months before you released your AI model."

"What are you suggesting?"

"I can't imagine that your partnership ended amicably. Did he help you develop the technology that made you rich?"

"You watch too many documentaries. This wasn't Bill Gates against Steve Jobs."

"He was your most talented worker. Why would you let someone like Mercer go?"

Saunders sighed and leaned against the car. "Ian Mercer had more bravado than talent. Let that be a lesson to you, Mr. Hopkins. Never let conceit come between you and your performance."

LeVar swallowed a retort. Despite the break-in, Saunders didn't appreciate the danger he was in.

"Can we leave?" Saunders asked.

"Lead the way."

32

Thomas awakened before dawn and pulled on his sweatpants. He descended the stairs and brewed tea while Jack and Tigger continued to snore in bed. He would have tossed on running sneakers and jogged a few miles like Chelsey, but he was a wimp about chilly temperatures. At the end of March, it was common for temperatures to fall into the teens during the early morning, and this was one such day.

Emma slept in the guest room. The woman finally seemed comfortable after spending the last few days apologizing for the intrusion. Give her a few weeks, and she might become one of the family like LeVar and the Mournings.

As he sipped the tea, he glanced over the list she'd worked on with Scout. These were message-board posters apparently a little too interested in catching the child abductor who terrorized Upstate New York and portions of New England and Pennsylvania. Was the killer among them? He had a sneaking suspicion that the man was, yet he couldn't explain why. Neither could he say why Nolan Trevino's videotapes drew his attention.

Which reminded him—he needed to bring a copy of Nolan's recordings to the tech lab. They would clean up the picture and get a better look at the man hiding amidst the trees. True, it was highly unlikely that the killer had wandered through Nolan's camera lens, but Thomas had little to go on and needed a break.

At the station, Aguilar was the first to greet him. She was making something in the blender, and he scurried past before she tested another one of her science-project smoothies on him.

"Morning, Thomas," Lambert said, entering a few minutes later. His red eyes spoke of poor sleep.

"Hey there, Lambert. You doing okay?"

"Nightmare."

Thomas raised an eyebrow. "You don't normally open up about nightmares."

"Don't get used to it," Lambert said, placing his keys in his desk drawer.

"It must have been a doozy."

"I was in a cemetery surrounded by trees. It reminded me of that place where the Hartleys told me to go. All these skeletal hands reached out of the ground and grabbed my ankles. It was terrible."

"What did you eat before bed?"

"Pasta with red sauce."

"A lot of food before sleep will give you nightmares," said Thomas.

"Is that true?"

"Thomas speaks the truth," Aguilar said. She gave Lambert a death stare. "How many times do I have to tell you to go easy on your body? You can't stuff yourself so late in the day."

"No choice." Lambert burped into a cupped hand. "I didn't get home until after nine."

"So you ate like a pig and missed out on sleep. It figures that you had bad dreams."

Thomas forced himself not to laugh. Whenever Aguilar

cornered Lambert, he acted like a scolded child who'd done wrong.

"Speaking of nightmares," Thomas said, "we still have a child killer to catch."

Aguilar grimaced. "I haven't forgotten."

"First thing we need to do is go through Emma and Scout's list again and zero in on three or four suspects. Then we'll do our best to trace them to their IP addresses. That means we'll have to concentrate our efforts on recent posts."

"The people who are raising a fuss about the vigil?" Lambert asked.

"That's correct. Emma will help you when she arrives. Remember, we're searching for a kidnapper, not a killer, whenever she's around."

"She must know this guy is a child murderer," Aguilar said.

"Emma is intelligent, but we need to consider her state of mind. The trauma she went through would bring us to our knees."

"No question about it."

Lambert belched again, and Aguilar rolled her eyes.

"Follow me to the break room," she told her fellow deputy.

"Oh, no," Lambert protested. "If you think I'll drink a gross-looking smoothie, you're wrong."

"Don't argue with me. I know just the recipe for settling an upset stomach."

Lambert looked at Thomas for help, but the sheriff just threw up his hands and wandered into his office. Down the hallway, Maggie entered the station and started her workday.

Thomas scanned through Nolan's footage while the blender whirred. His deputies were arguing, but it was impossible to hear over the clamor. While he waited for the mysterious stranger to return to the park, the racket in the breakroom ended. Now his deputies were discussing Emma's list. Lambert stopped burping. As usual, Aguilar was right.

The stranger didn't show up on the other recordings. That was a problem because the only picture he had of the man was shadowed and grainy.

"Boss man," Lambert said with a rap on the door. "We have three names worth looking into."

Thomas was more than happy to step away from the videos, which kept making his head spin. They convened at the center table. Now that Lambert's stomach issues had ceased, Aguilar wore an I-told-you-so expression.

"What names stuck out to you?" Thomas asked.

Aguilar read the first two names. Both posters had discussed the abductions during the late 1990s and involved themselves in the recent debates.

Lambert tapped his finger against the page. "But one guy really stands out. His name is Adrian Castell. Get this. Castell lived in Wolf Lake through 1999 before leaving. He recently moved back and bought a place on the edge of the village."

"Where did he live during the last two decades?"

"Here and there. Seems he doesn't like to stay in one spot."

"Pennsylvania and Massachusetts?"

"Among other places. Until last month, he lived fifteen miles north of Elko, Nevada. I'm searching the database for similar abductions in Nevada."

"Criminal record?"

"Clean as a whistle."

"All that means is he's too smart for the police to catch him," Aguilar said.

"Until now."

Thomas nodded. This might be their guy. "Do you have a photograph?"

"We do," Aguilar said. She loaded the suspect's driver's

license. "Good-looking man. Smile appears genuine and nonthreatening. I can see how he might win a child's trust."

"Slow down. We need more evidence to call him a serial killer."

"How is this for you?" Lambert asked. The deputy passed a printout across the table. "Background check on Mr. Castell."

Thomas skimmed through the important details. "Parents divorced when he was four. Lived with his father until the age of eleven."

"Correct. The father went to prison after the police discovered he'd raped seven women."

Thomas recalled the profile from the Behavioral Analysis Unit. Everything fit so far.

"Major trauma occurred when he was the same age as our missing girls."

"Plus," Aguilar said, "he learned to objectify women from his rapist father."

"Good God. This is tremendous work, both of you. Here's what I want you to do next."

"Sheriff, there are two people waiting to see you."

At the sound of Maggie's voice, Thomas spun to face his administrative assistant.

"Can you tell them to leave a message? We're swamped trying to solve the Hannah Clarke investigation."

"They say it can't wait. It's Trish Harris's parents."

Trish had sworn someone chased her and her friends through the abandoned home near their school.

Thomas glanced at his deputies before responding. "Okay, send them in."

Maggie escorted the Harris couple inside. The father clutched a phone, and the mother hooked elbows with her husband, as if afraid a sudden wind might tear them apart.

"Sheriff," the man said, "this might be nothing, but I wanted you to decide for yourself."

Mr. Harris handed Thomas a phone adorned with a young girl's stickers. A picture of the village park filled the screen.

"It's important because of what happened at that ghost house," Mrs. Harris said. "With all the talk around Wolf Lake about child predators, we wanted you to see this picture."

Thomas stared at the image. A man stood behind the tree line, just as the stranger had in Nolan's video. The unknown person was watching children play. "When did Trish take this image?"

"The day before they trespassed," Mr. Harris said. "The timestamp is on the picture."

After enlarging the image, Thomas couldn't say for sure that this was the same man from the video, let alone Adrian Castell.

"I need this photograph. Can you forward it to me?"

Mr. Harris handed the phone to his wife, who demonstrated how to share the picture with Thomas and his deputies. The image arrived, and Aguilar took the couple to her desk for additional details.

Outside the window, Chelsey walked Emma to the entry doors.

Thomas lowered his voice. "Lambert, send this picture and a still frame from Nolan Trevino's video to the tech lab. Have them clean the images and lighten the shadows. If it's the same guy, I need to know."

33

The community college in Harmon canceled its afternoon classes after a water main broke and filled two education buildings with several inches of flooding. Sometimes fate worked in your favor.

With the rest of his day free, LeVar set up a coordination call with Raven and Chelsey. They were tag-teaming their efforts so they could follow Elliot Saunders, who was jumping from one location to the next, as if the technologist weren't facing an unseen threat. That freed LeVar to set his sights on Ian Mercer.

He parked in a lot beside the apartment complex where Mercer lived. The view of the exit doors guaranteed nobody would come or go without LeVar knowing. Now it was a matter of watching and waiting. He enjoyed surveillance missions but preferred a partner to bounce ideas off. Or at least someone to keep him company.

An Erik B and Rakim track played inside his Chrysler Limited. He kept the volume low so it didn't distract him from the surrounding environment. Through a pair of binoculars, he glimpsed a silhouette cross a window in Mercer's apartment. The shade was drawn.

He looked out the window when a tractor trailer rumbled by. It took the corner too fast and got stuck, blocking traffic. The inevitable chorus of horns began.

While he waited for Mercer to make a move, LeVar rechecked the suspect's background. Saunders' rival fit LeVar's profile to a T. All along, he'd believed a business rival was stalking their client. But until Mercer showed his hand, it was all conjecture.

"You have your radio on?" asked Raven through the walkie-talkie.

"Right here, sis. What you got for me?"

"Chelsey and I are about to finish up with Saunders. His last appearance of the day fell through, so he's driving back to the Harmon office. He swears he won't leave until we return and escort him to his buddy's house."

"So nice of Mr. Happy Pants to cooperate."

"You're not a fan, I take it."

"I respect his intelligence, but something tells me he really did Mercer dirty."

"Never forgive the guilty party because he got a raw deal."

LeVar looked in the mirror and worked a piece of dental floss between his teeth. He shouldn't have bought that bag of popcorn at the community college's dining hall.

"I'm not, but remember the deets you gave me about his background. If anything, Mercer has a stronger resume than Saunders. This guy should be on top of the AI world, but according to your findings, he drives part-time for a package delivery company."

"Not everyone with a strong resume gets their dream job."

"Trust me. This guy got the shaft, and now he wants payback. And you know what they say about payback?"

Raven laughed. "Keep the communication G-rated. Scout

will continue to research the stalker at Wolf Lake Consulting, just in case we're wrong about Mercer."

He pictured the girl at the office, probably wearing another outfit that would make a guy check her out. But not him. He had to be careful and keep things platonic.

"She's there alone?"

"Darren took a few hours off from the state park so he could watch over her. Plus, he's coordinating with a few buddies from his Syracuse PD days. They're feeding him everything they have on Mercer and Saunders."

"*Aight.*"

Chelsey's voice came through the speaker. "Hey, LeVar?"

"Right here, Chelsey."

"How long has Mercer been inside his apartment?"

"Since I arrived an hour ago. Can't say where he was beforehand. Why?"

"It's weird that he didn't show up at Saunders' engagements. He's lying low."

"He's planning something," said LeVar.

"That's what worries me."

At the window, a hand grabbed the shade and gave it a tug, letting daylight into the apartment. There was Mercer, looking out at the city. To LeVar, it appeared as if the man were searching the sidewalk, looking for someone. Like a cop or a private investigator?

"Hold up, Chelsey. He might be on the move."

Mercer reached down and grabbed something off a table. He slid the object into his pocket.

Keys or a weapon?

The man turned and presented his profile to the world as he fixed his hair in the mirror. Then he walked past and headed for the door.

"Lost sight of him," LeVar said. "I think he's walking toward the exit."

"If he leaves," Raven said, "follow him."

"You don't have to ask."

LeVar turned the key in the ignition and waited inside the idling car. Traffic passed, blocking his view of the doors. One second, all he could see was a minivan. The next, Ian Mercer jumped off the curb and aimed a key fob at a beat-up black sports car with a dented rear bumper. LeVar had no time to duck. Mercer's vehicle was only three spots from his.

For a frozen heartbeat, the two men locked eyes. LeVar lifted his chin and grinned, then cranked the volume. The bass drum of the hip-hop made his teeth rattle. He bobbed his head to the beat and pretended to read his phone.

Mercer didn't give him a second glance. The suspect climbed into the sports car, gunned the engine, and shot off in a black cloud of exhaust.

Stupid.

LeVar chided himself for allowing Mercer to spot him. At least the man didn't suspect someone was following.

"Heading west of Montour Street," LeVar said into the walkie-talkie.

"Any idea where he's heading?" Chelsey asked.

"I-481, if I had to guess. Then he'll pick up I-81 and drive to Harmon."

"So you think he's coming toward us?"

"Toward Saunders, yeah. Don't move from your spot. I have a bad feeling about this."

LeVar drummed his fingers on his thighs with impatience. When Mercer was ahead enough, he left the parking lot and followed. As he expected, Saunders' stalker turned on his blinker and merged onto the I-481 on ramp.

Now the two vehicles raced down the highway at 70 mph,

with LeVar five cars behind his quarry and hoping the man didn't spot him in the mirror. Mercer weaved from one lane to the next, as if he were late for an engagement. An unscheduled appointment with Saunders, LeVar assumed.

"He hopped on I-81," he said into the radio. "Be ready. This guy seems pretty determined."

Chelsey acknowledged the report as LeVar passed a tour bus. He needed to keep Mercer in sight.

The afternoon commute clogged the interstate by the time Harmon came into view. It was no surprise when the stalking suspect took the exit and entered the city.

Beneath the ramp, the city's disenfranchised wandered about. A man pushed a shopping cart stuffed with cans and bottles. Two miniskirt-wearing underage girls stood outside the adult video store. This used to be 315 Royals territory before LeVar and Harmon PD rounded up the last of the thugs.

Eight blocks ahead, the slums gave way to the heart of the city. Skyscrapers towered above the city traffic. A glowing soft-drink sign hung off a high-rise.

"Where is he now?" Raven asked.

"Mercer took a left on Second Street. He should reach your position in two minutes."

There was no doubt about the suspect's destination. Elliot Saunders' office lay dead ahead.

"Copy that."

"When he hits the intersection of Main and Fifth, pull out behind him. I'm afraid he'll see me in the mirror and get suspicious."

After Chelsey's Honda Civic took LeVar's position in the chase, he released a breath and stopped at the curb. Cars buzzed past, some beeping. He stared through the windshield at the high-tech building where Saunders worked. His AI firm leased the first-floor offices.

"Coming back your way," Chelsey announced.

"He's circling the block, isn't he?"

He didn't need Chelsey to confirm what he already knew. Mercer was canvassing Saunders. And planning what?

Mercer rounded the block three times.

"Next time around," LeVar said, "pull over so I can take your place."

"Gotcha."

His legs bounced as he observed the procession through the mirrors. Mercer was stuck at a red light, with Chelsey and Raven three vehicles behind.

"Don't recognize me, bro," LeVar said to the suspect's reflection.

The light turned green. As Chelsey's Civic stopped in a parking lot, there came Mercer. LeVar placed his foot over the accelerator, ready to shoot off the curb and fight his way into traffic.

Except Mercer didn't pass.

Tires screeched. The suspect stopped in a towaway zone.

"Something is happening," LeVar said into the radio.

Mercer climbed out of the vehicle without looking. A honking pickup almost ran him down. The suspect didn't seem to notice. Saunders' rival reached into his back pocket and removed a black object.

LeVar prayed it was a wallet. It wasn't.

He had a second to yell, "Gun!" into the radio before screams rang out.

34

Pedestrians scrambled for cover. Some dove onto the sidewalk.

Gun in hand, Ian Mercer stomped across the street, heading straight at the building where Saunders worked.

Criminal profiles were theoretical. Sometimes they nailed the suspect. Other times, they led you astray. But everything had added up this time. Ian Mercer had developed a professional rivalry with Elliot Saunders, though LeVar didn't know the details. Somehow, Saunders had hurt Mercer and destroyed his career. Now the former employee wanted to exact revenge.

From the corner of his eye, LeVar saw Chelsey and Raven sprinting from the Civic to get into position. They drew their weapons, but it was too late. A crowd stood between them and the suspect. Only LeVar had a bead on the man. In the back of his mind, he realized he wasn't on duty and wearing Kevlar. If Mercer turned his gun on him, he was as good as dead.

As LeVar dodged speeding cars, he yelled into his police radio. He needed backup, but there was no chance Harmon PD would arrive before the unthinkable happened.

Please don't let Mercer open fire on a bunch of innocents.

The suspect appeared not to notice anyone around him. He strode forward as people lunged out of his path.

More screams. Up the steps, silhouetted figures stood in the lobby inside Saunders' firm. Was the AI guru among them?

"Ian Mercer, freeze! Nightshade County Sheriff's Department!"

The shooter didn't hear or didn't care. He lifted the gun and aimed it at someone behind the glass.

No more time.

LeVar struck Mercer from the side. A surprised grunt came from the armed man. The gun tumbled and clanged against the concrete steps as LeVar lifted his quarry by the legs and took him down.

The suspect's eyes widened upon recognizing LeVar. They wrestled on the steps, rolling over as they battled for the top position. Mercer was stronger than expected. But not as strong as LeVar.

"Don't fight back," the deputy said. "I don't want to hurt you."

Mercer kept struggling. He pushed his arms up and attempted to toss LeVar off him. Not today. LeVar shifted his weight and kept him down.

As people yelled for help, LeVar stayed on top of his thrashing foe and grabbed his hands. Then Raven and Chelsey arrived.

"He's not worth it, Mercer."

Hearing his name shocked the gunman back to reality. He looked up at LeVar.

"Whatever Saunders did to you, he's not worth spending the rest of your life in jail."

"He stole everything from me," Mercer said. "That AI model

that made him millions—I developed it. All he did was make a few minor adjustments and call it his own. Elliot Saunders is nothing but a crook."

"You'll have your chance to tell the world."

Mercer wasn't done fighting.

"Grab the gun," LeVar said, cocking his head toward the fallen weapon.

Raven retrieved Mercer's gun while Chelsey pinned the man's legs to keep him still. From his back pocket, LeVar removed a pair of handcuffs. After clamping them on Mercer's wrists, he could finally breathe. A few blocks away, police sirens rose and fell. Help was on the way.

"Over here," Raven said when the officers stopped beside the road. She motioned them forward.

Unsure if the police officers would recognize him, LeVar reached into his pocket and displayed his deputy badge. The first two officers who arrived acknowledged him. As the others swooped in, Mercer stopped struggling.

Raven kneeled beside her brother. "I overheard. It sounds like Saunders isn't such a nice guy after all."

"Remember my profile? The stalker worked with Saunders."

"And now we know Mercer wasn't any old worker. He had the skills to run Saunders' company."

The flashing lights of the police cruisers swept across their faces. With the situation under control, Harmon PD divided its efforts; the two lead officers read Mercer his rights while the others kept the crowd from advancing. The police hauled up Mercer and walked him to a cruiser with an open door. The madness had ended.

"What's the situation?" the lead officer asked.

LeVar briefed him. "Wolf Lake Consulting was handling a stalking case involving Elliot Saunders, the man who works inside the building. The gunman is Ian Mercer. It seems the two men developed a rivalry over an application they developed."

"And Mercer wanted to solve the issue by shooting his enemy? Figures."

"Not that I'm excusing Mercer's behavior," Raven said, "but it appears Saunders stole Mercer's technology. The application is worth seven figures. Maybe more."

The officer whistled. "This is one for the gossip sheets."

As Raven told the officer everything she knew about Mercer, Saunders rushed out of the building. His face was ashen.

"Is that who I think it is?" Saunders asked.

"Ian Mercer, your former partner."

The AI developer grimaced. "He was never my partner, just a wannabe who couldn't admit his designs were too flawed to bring to the marketplace."

"You held back the truth," Chelsey said, giving Saunders a disapproving look. "Had you told us about Mercer on day one, we could have deescalated the situation before it spun out of control."

"And kept you safe," Raven added.

Saunders placed his hands on his hips. "How could I predict Mercer would lose his mind and attempt to destroy everything I worked for?"

"You mean everything both of you worked for?"

"No, the technology is mine. Wait until the truth comes out. Ian Mercer is a fraud."

"Take Saunders inside," the lead officer said. "He's bugging me."

The second officer, a man named Harper, placed a hand on LeVar's shoulder. "Okay, deputy. I'll need a full debriefing. Same with you, Chelsey and Raven."

"Whatever you need," LeVar said. He jogged down the steps

and found a quiet spot away from the crowd so he and Harper could speak. “Ask me your questions, dawg.”

“Begin with when you knew Mercer intended to open fire on Saunders.”

LeVar took a moment to collect his thoughts, still feeling the adrenaline from the confrontation. Officer Harper waited, his notebook ready.

"*Aight*, from the top. I trailed Mercer from his apartment in Fayetteville, not knowing things would go so far. He drove to Harmon and circled the block. It was clear he was targeting Saunders' building. Then everything went haywire."

"And you were armed?"

"Correct. I was off duty, acting in my capacity with Wolf Lake Consulting. But I couldn't stand by." LeVar looked towards the cruiser where Mercer was now detained. "When he drew his weapon, I knew I had to act as a county deputy. I caught him on the steps and tackled him before he could fire a shot."

Raven, who hadn’t started her debriefing yet, approached. "LeVar's quick thinking saved lives today. Had it not been for him, innocents might have died."

Harper looked up from his notes. "And the takedown?"

"It was all instinct," LeVar said. "We struggled, but I disarmed him. Then, with Raven and Chelsey's help, we secured him until you guys arrived."

Harper closed his notebook. "Helluva job, LeVar. This could have gotten ugly fast, and you prevented a massacre. We'll take it from here. How’s the sheriff?"

“You know how he rolls, Harper. Got a million things on his mind, and he still manages it all.”

“Is he close to solving that cold case? That goes back, what, to the 1990s?”

“Once Shep Dawg gets on the trail, he never stops sniffing.”

Officer Harper turned his attention to the building and

sighed. “I suppose I need to deal with this prima donna now. We'll get statements from the witnesses. Thanks for your help, LeVar, Chelsey, Raven. This could have been much worse.”

As Harper climbed the steps, they watched Saunders stroll away from the window. Though LeVar could only make out the man’s silhouette, he appeared shaken and defeated. When the truth about the rivalry reached the press, the story might paint Saunders in an unkind light. If half of what Mercer said was true, Saunders deserved an undressing.

For LeVar, the day had taken an unexpected turn. The confrontation with Ian Mercer, the rush of adrenaline, and the sudden responsibility of having to pull double duty as a consultant and a deputy drove home how unpredictable law enforcement was.

Raven wore a scowl. "What now? Saunders isn't exactly innocent."

LeVar holstered his service weapon. "We did what we could. The rest is up to the legal system. But we need to finish what we started with Saunders. After Harmon PD talks to him, I want more information. If he stole Mercer’s technology, maybe we can prove it."

“I can't believe Saunders didn't mention any of this,” said Chelsey. “He played us, making us think he was a victim.”

"Let’s face it. Not every dude we defend is a boy scout."

“Today, we prevented a tragedy,” Raven said. “That's what matters. If Saunders is a dirt bag, it’s not up to us to judge. And hey, he paid us for our services.”

Chelsey grinned. “I appreciate you for finding the silver lining. After all the financial issues Wolf Lake Consulting faced in the past, it’s nice to be profitable again. And I have you to thank.”

Raven’s eyes glassed over.

"What about me?" LeVar asked. "I'm the one who laid the smack down on Mercer."

"But you brought down our profit margins."

"How's that? Y'all don't pay me."

"Donuts, LeVar. You know much a dozen costs these days?"

"Chelsey has you there," Raven said.

LeVar harrumphed. "I don't get no respect."

35

"I haven't heard from the tech lab."

Thomas blew out a breath of frustration as Lambert provided an update. Earlier today, they'd sent two images—one from Trish Harris's phone, the other from Nolan Trevino's videotape—to the tech lab. He needed those images cleaned, brightened, sharpened. Anything they could do to give him a better look at the man in the park.

"Call them again," Thomas said. "They close in an hour, and I need those images before everyone leaves for the day."

Lambert got back on the phone while Aguilar worked with Emma at her desk. On an open laptop, Adrian Castell's driver's license photo continued to stare at Thomas. Was this their killer?

The sheriff busied himself with the last of Nolan's recordings. Lambert appeared in the door with a relieved look.

"The lab sent the images to both our emails. You should have them now."

Thomas shut off the VHS player and opened his mail client. The digital images were slow to load because the lab hadn't compressed them. He set the two pictures side by side and slid his chair closer to the screen. Lambert craned his neck over the sheriff's shoulder.

The pictures weren't perfect, but facial features appeared where there had been only shadows and noise this morning. Comparing the two figures to a picnic table in the background, Thomas tapped the screen.

"Similar height and build. This might be the same guy."

Lambert squinted. "Maybe. It's tough to tell. Zoom in."

Thomas did. Now he could see the faces, though a touch of blur concealed both.

"I'll be damned. The figure in the Harris picture is older, but a few decades have passed since Nolan Trevino shot his footage. I can buy that they're one and the same."

"Thomas, I might be overthinking things, but doesn't the more recent image remind you of Adrian Castell?"

"It does. We might have found our murderer."

Before Lambert let out a whoop, Thomas pointed at Emma. The deputy understood. For the journalist, this was an unspeakable tragedy. Celebrating would send the wrong message.

"I want more information on Castell," Thomas said. "Everything he's been up to since he moved back to Wolf Lake. Where does he hang out? Who are his friends? If this guy so much as sneezes, I want to know."

"I'll put two deputies on Castell."

"Plain-clothed. Make sure they remain discreet."

Lambert hurried out of the office as Thomas wrestled with indecision. Aguilar needed an update, but should he tell Emma? He didn't want to raise her hopes. Adrian Castell sure looked like the guy in the park, but even if he were, that didn't prove he had killed Hannah. Still, it was a darn big step.

A theory came to him. They'd run a search on a pair of fingerprints lifted from the empty house. The man to whom they belonged wasn't in AFIS. A quick search confirmed that Adrian Castell wasn't in the system either. And the profile fit.

For days, Thomas and his team had pored over records of convicts in the prison system, but their unsub had been free all this time. It was possible Castell had never stopped killing. Because he moved around, the murders didn't form patterns. That kept law enforcement from closing in.

Until now.

"Sheriff, you have two visitors."

Maggie stood in the doorway.

"Not again, Maggie. We're too busy to meet with the public."

"It's the Hartleys, the folks Deputy Lambert helped after their tire blew."

"What do they want?"

"All they said was it was important. The woman—Clara is her name?—says she has information you need to hear."

Thomas didn't have time for this, not now. But it didn't seem like the Hartleys would leave without talking to him.

"I'll meet them at the table. Give me two minutes."

Thomas checked his reflection on the screen and straightened his hair. He would make this quick and send James and Clara on their way. Then he would focus on Adrian Castell.

Upon exiting his office, he painted a smile on his face and acted as if nothing serious were happening. The public couldn't learn that they were closing in on a murder suspect.

"Mr. and Mrs. Hartley. How can I assist you today?"

Clara cupped her elbows with her hands and stared out the window. James gave his wife a frustrated glance and turned to him.

"I'm so sorry to bother you with this, Sheriff, but my wife—"

"I saw that man in the woods," she said.

Thomas crinkled his brow. "What man?"

"The hunter . . . or whoever it was that chased us through the forest. The man with the gun."

"Where did you see him?"

"Same place as before. I had to come into Wolf Lake on business this afternoon, so I took the back road where we'd blown a tire. There was a man watching me from the trees as I drove past. It had to be the same guy."

Thomas stepped closer. "Did you identify him?"

Clara's face fell, and James rolled his eyes.

"She doesn't know who she saw," James said. "It could have been anyone."

Clara stomped down. "It. Was. Him."

Thomas spotted Lambert watching the conversation. Nobody should be in those woods. He didn't want to waste time chasing after a stranger, but if this guy was running around with a gun, the sheriff's department needed to intervene.

"Easy, folks," Thomas said. "What if you showed me exactly where you saw him? My deputy and I will check it out."

"And there were unmarked graves on top of that hill. I swear they were there."

In the background, Lambert shrugged a shoulder.

The Hannah Clarke cold case was his priority, but Thomas had to follow up on Clara's claims. On a printed map, the woman confirmed the location.

"All right, folks. I'll check the forest and tell you what I find."

Lambert escorted the husband and wife out of the building. Thomas briefed Aguilar on his plans.

A short walk later, he found Lambert waiting beside the cruiser. It was obvious the deputy had reservations about wasting time in the forest. Not to mention they were running out of daylight.

When the location came into view, Thomas scanned the

shoulder for tire tracks. A car had parked along the road and driven off.

"Here we are," Lambert said, killing the engine.

The deputy led him up the hill, which was even steeper than expected. His boots struggled to find footing. At times, it seemed like he was looking straight up into an abyss.

"Not much farther," the deputy said. "But I'm telling you, Thomas: I found the clearing, and there were no crosses or unmarked graves. When people experience stress, they don't think straight."

Thomas didn't respond. He struggled to keep his breath.

When they reached the top, Lambert grabbed his arm and helped him over the edge. The dense, dark forest opened into a clearing. A blood-red sky hung overhead.

"This isn't right," Lambert said. "None of this was here before."

Thomas stared. Before them, rows of crosses stuck out of the earth like bony fingers. They were fashioned with sticks and twine.

There had to be a dozen crosses. No, two dozen.

What lay beneath the symbols?

Lambert swallowed. "Thomas, how many children disappeared from Nightshade County?"

Thomas stepped forward. Now he stood among the symbols. They seemed to accuse him of not helping, of not doing more.

"Call the New York State Police," Thomas said. "Tell them to bring LIDAR."

36

"None of this was here before, Thomas. I swear."

Lambert spun in a circle. Around him, the spindly crosses formed a macabre barrier.

"I know they weren't," Thomas said. He donned gloves and kneeled beside one cross. It pulled out of the ground with ease. "Someone removed these the first time you surveyed the clearing."

Thomas knew the reason. This was a gravesite, and their mystery hunter, or whoever the man was, didn't want anyone to know.

They heard the state trooper cruisers arrive. From the clearing, it was impossible to see down the hill.

"Keep your eyes open," said Thomas. "This guy might still be around."

The more time the sheriff stood among the crosses, the sicker he felt. If he didn't compose himself, what lay beneath the surface would break him. His radio squawked as the troopers relayed their position.

Trooper Fitzgerald was leading the team, and Thomas could

hear a cadaver dog scraping through the underbrush. If Thomas's guess was correct, Fitzgerald was courting Aguilar, though now wasn't the time to consider such thoughts.

Lambert kept watch over the woods, ready if the stranger who'd stalked the Hartleys showed his face. But the first people to come out of the forest were the New York State Troopers. A cushioned case hung off Fitzgerald's shoulder.

"Thomas," Fitzgerald said. "What do we have here?"

Thomas gestured at the crosses. "I'm not sure I want to find out."

"Are those for real?" another trooper asked.

"God, I hope not."

Fitzgerald joined a junior trooper before the crosses; the ground was uneven and dotted with patches of long, untamed grass. Lambert shifted his weight from one foot to the other, glancing at the equipment Fitzgerald had unloaded from his patrol car.

"So, you really think you can find . . . you know, if there's anything buried here?" Lambert asked.

Fitzgerald patted the case that housed the LIDAR unit. "Absolutely. LIDAR—Light Detection and Ranging—uses laser pulses to map out the surface of the ground. It's like radar, but with light. We lean on LIDAR to detect changes in the land that aren't visible to the naked eye."

"We used it during my military days, but I've never searched for bodies."

"When someone is buried, it changes the composition of the soil. Over time, as decomposition sets in, it can cause the ground above to settle differently than the surrounding area. LIDAR can pick up the subtle differences."

"Right. It shoots lasers into the ground and the light bounces back, giving us a picture of what's underneath."

"Exactly," Fitzgerald said. He opened the case and revealed

the device. "But it's more about the surface than deep underground. We look for irregularities in the ground level. Then, if we find something that looks off, we can dig to investigate further."

The cadaver dog tugged on her leash. "And we have this good girl to help," the junior deputy holding the leash said.

Lambert moaned. "This is something straight out of a horror movie."

That statement silenced the others. Even the dog stopped tugging at his leash.

"Shall we begin, Thomas?" Fitzgerald asked.

As Thomas stepped forward, another voice came through his radio. He recognized Aguilar, but distortion prevented him from making out what she'd said.

"Come again, Aguilar?"

The trees rustled. A shape burst out of the darkness. At once, the officers turned their weapons on the figure.

"Hold up," Thomas said, incredulous. "She's one of us."

What was Emma doing here?

A second later, Aguilar rushed into the clearing and sent Thomas an apologetic look. "I tried to stop her, Thomas, but she took off as soon as your radio call came in."

"Emma," said Thomas, approaching the trembling woman with caution. "Why are you here?"

Yet he knew the reason. She'd heard about this horrific cemetery and come to the same conclusion—all those missing girls were here. As was Hannah.

"We can't say for sure," he said.

"I know who's buried in the clearing," Emma said. "Can't you feel it?"

He could. The others watched without replying. If his suspicions were correct, this was the worst nightmare he'd ever faced.

Thomas bit his lip and turned to Fitzgerald. "Show me."

As the sun fell, fog formed and weaved through the brush in ghostly tendrils. Beside them, the cadaver dog strained at his leash, eager to begin his search. The LIDAR equipment stood on a tripod. It hummed quietly when the trooper powered on the device.

"All right, Thomas, we're all set here," Fitzgerald said. "Once I start the scan, Sadie will do her part. Between the LIDAR and her training, if there's anything to find, we'll locate it."

And by anything, Fitzgerald meant rows of children. No, it couldn't be true.

"We're losing light. Better get started."

Fitzgerald tapped a few commands into his laptop and initiated the LIDAR scan. A whirring sound filled the air as the device emitted rapid pulses of light, invisible to the naked eye, which swept over the terrain.

Sadie's holder guided the cadaver dog along the clearing's perimeter. The dog darted from point to point with her nose to the ground, while Fitzgerald kept his eyes glued to the laptop, watching as the landscape was rendered on the screen.

"See this area here?" Fitzgerald pointed to a section on the screen where the ground's texture appeared irregular. "That could be something. The soil's disturbed, not matching the natural lay of the land."

Thomas studied the display. "How accurate is this?"

"Very. But Sadie's reaction will tell us more. If there's decomposition, she'll pick up on it."

As if on cue, the dog started barking and pawing at the ground near the disturbed area. The handler tried to calm her, but the dog was persistent, digging and whining.

"That tells me we have a body," Fitzgerald said. "Sadie has a solid track record. We should mark this spot for the forensic team."

Confirmation. And Fitzgerald had only focused the LIDAR on one grave marker. How many more?

Thomas glanced at Emma, who covered her mouth and turned away. The woman's knees buckled. He signaled at Aguilar to check on her.

Fitzgerald said, "We'll need to be careful how we proceed. Any excavation has to preserve the evidence."

The lead trooper lifted the tripod and carried it several feet to the next marking. A knot formed in Thomas's stomach. Sadie waited to the side.

Fitzgerald adjusted the equipment. "We're looking for another anomaly under the ground. Areas where someone disturbed the soil and then filled in will reflect the laser differently. If LIDAR picks up anything suspicious, we'll let Sadie do her work again."

The machine beeped, and Fitzgerald peered at the screen, analyzing the data streaming in real time. The LIDAR revealed another anomaly beneath the surface. As the state trooper worked, Thomas ran his vision over the forest's edge. Was the madman who'd done this watching them now?

Before Thomas could send the other troopers to canvas the area, Fitzgerald said, "Looks like we have something. Go ahead, Sadie."

With a purposeful bark, Sadie moved towards the marked area. Her nose skimmed the ground. The others watched in silence as the dog circled, then pawed at the earth, her tail wagging.

Fitzgerald looked at Thomas, a solemn understanding passing between them. "Let's dig here," he said.

"We'll need a forensics team and the medical examiner. Aguilar, could you—"

He stopped when he saw Aguilar looking around, confused. Dusk had fallen. Where was Emma?

"She was right beside me," Aguilar said. "I don't know where she went."

"Emma!"

Thomas's call went unanswered.

37

Her focus was on Hannah. As always.

But the second Emma saw all those child-sized bodies show up on the sensing equipment, she turned and ran. The horror was too much to bear.

Where she'd run to, she could only guess. Forest surrounded her. Her shoulder struck a tree as she stumbled blindly. So dark. So much pain.

Her stomach gurgled. She placed her hands on her knees and became sick in the underbrush.

Emma was certain Hannah was among the victims. And there were so many. Dozens. Perhaps more.

She wiped spittle from her lips with the back of her hand. Her breaths came too quickly, and she realized she would hyperventilate and pass out if she didn't regain control.

The conversation with Hannah replayed in her mind—the girl had wanted to become a journalist someday. Why had Emma laughed at her friend? And why hadn't she followed the girl to the store?

Her hand touched her pocket, and that's when she realized

the phone wasn't there. Damn. It must have toppled out of her coat while she ran.

Foolish.

She rested against a tree and thought again about her last conversation with Hannah. In her mind, she would always picture her friend turning the corner and disappearing. That was the last time anyone had seen the girl.

Except for the psychopath who'd stolen Hannah and killed her like the others.

A bird squawked in the tree. She looked around, aware that she'd run too far. No longer could she hear the police officers. By now, they were searching for her.

Somewhere, a branch crackled under a heavy weight. Her back went ramrod straight.

Was the killer in these woods? Unless he was a fool, the man had run the second all those cruisers stopped outside the forest. Logic told Emma she was alone. Her instinct said she wasn't.

Slowly, carefully, she peered out from behind the tree. The forest was pitch-black, with the canopy shutting out the moon and stars.

"Sheriff?"

She prayed the noise she'd heard was Thomas Shepherd. The sheriff would have called out to her, right?

Going quiet, she listened. A long way off, a voice shouted. Probably an officer looking for her. Though Emma had lost her way, if she followed the shout to its source, she would find the police.

But abandoning her position felt wrong. Dangerous.

An Eagles song came from the forest. Her ringtone. The phone was near.

Finding the phone seemed worth the risk, so she stepped out from behind the tree and walked toward the sound. When she closed in, the song stopped.

She got down on her hands and knees and parted the brush, heedless of the thorns and prickers that tore her flesh. What if the sheriff had called her?

Reaching into the brush, she touched something slick and spongy. Her hand snapped back, and she recoiled. A dead bird. Something had torn out the bird's throat.

When the song started again, she swung her head to the side. The phone was somewhere to the left. That made sense. After she'd collided with the tree, the device must have fallen out of her coat.

"Emma!"

Thomas Shepherd's voice. Where?

She stood and stared, but all she saw was infinite darkness.

The bushes rattled. Emma spun and reached into her pocket for a weapon that wasn't there. Another mistake. She never should have come here without first arming herself.

"Thomas, is that you?"

The hand closed around her mouth and shut off her air supply. Red-hot panic lanced through her body.

She bit the assailant's thumb and refused to let go.

Something struck the back of her head. Her eyes rolled. When her knees gave out, she fell into a man's arms.

"My sweet," he whispered with fetid breath. "It has been too long."

38

"I want her found," Thomas said. "Now!"

Aguilar and Lambert fanned out and walked around the clearing's perimeter. The state police continued to interrogate the land, uncovering more horrific images of children's bodies hidden underground, but everyone had drawn a weapon.

Thomas couldn't accept that the killer had walked right into the clearing and taken Emma while their backs were turned. Impossible. She must have run off on her own, horrified by what the LIDAR displayed. Had she fled into the killer's arms?

He grabbed Trooper Fitzgerald's arm. "I have to find Emma Walsh. Can you run the show?"

"I'll handle the investigation. Take two of my officers to help with your search. And Sadie. Take her too."

"What about your job? Don't you need a cadaver dog?"

Fitzgerald chewed the corner of his mouth. "We both know what's buried here, Thomas. Sadie isn't a trained tracker, but she'll do in a pinch. If Emma is close, Sadie will find her."

A trooper took the leash and joined Thomas.

"Lambert, you know this forest as well as anyone."

"I've only been here once," Lambert said.

"We believe in you," said Aguilar.

If anyone could find a lost person in a dense forest, it was Tristan Lambert. He didn't need experience tracking people in these woods. His skills and instincts would take over.

As they entered the forest, a hand touched his back.

"Thomas, I should have watched her."

He looked at Aguilar. "It's not your fault. She ran away on her own."

The diminutive deputy raised a rock-solid chin. "When I find Emma, I'm attaching her to my arm with a rope. No way am I chasing after her again."

"We'll find her."

Dark forest stood to all sides. The steep terrain made it challenging to keep his footing. Walking alongside Lambert, the state trooper and Sadie led the team.

Thomas called to Emma. His voice echoed and died.

Would his phone work? The Hartleys had said they couldn't get a signal in the forest, but Thomas spied one fleeting bar on the display.

"Here goes nothing." He called the journalist's number, listening to it ring as he skidded downhill. "Come on, answer."

But she didn't.

"She came this way," Lambert said, pointing to a snapped twig that hung like a broken limb. "Follow me."

Thomas felt a surge of hope. Lambert would find Emma.

Flashlight beams lit trees and swept across the forest floor. Dead leaves crunched underfoot, and the mud sucked on his shoes. His pants had soaked beneath the knees, and the night was turning chilly.

"Anything?" asked Thomas.

"Over here." Lambert kneeled and gestured. "Shine your

light past my hand." The flashlight beam found a shoe print. "I'd say that came from a woman's shoe."

"Appears to be the right size," Aguilar said.

They were heading in the right direction, but it would only get darker. Thomas tried Emma's phone again and landed in the woman's voicemail. It was possible Emma's coverage wasn't as strong, but Thomas worried she'd hurt herself.

Or someone had found her.

Then Sadie let out a bark and tugged his handler sideways.

"Sadie has her scent," the trooper said.

With Lambert's intuition and the dog's nose in agreement, the team rushed forward, determined to rescue the lost journalist before the unthinkable happened. As Thomas jogged, he redialed.

Lambert stopped and held up a hand. Everyone fell quiet.

From the black, he heard *New Boy in Town*, an old Eagle's song.

"That's her ringtone," Aguilar said. "I heard it at the station."

Not worrying about the consequences, the team members ran on, trying to close the distance on the sound before the song stopped. Sadie barked.

"Emma, it's Sheriff Shepherd," Thomas yelled. "Call out to me. We'll come get you."

Why hadn't she replied?

Lambert dropped to his knees and lifted a glowing object. Thomas's heart sank. The deputy had found Emma's phone.

Beyond the forest, tires screeched.

"He's getting away!" Aguilar shouted.

The killer had taken Emma.

~

Three police vehicles drove the back roads in search of a killer. Thomas looked out the window while Lambert piloted the cruiser. Full night had fallen over Nightshade County.

"I want an armed checkpoint at every intersection within a three-mile radius of the forest," Thomas said into the radio.

Dispatch would forward his instructions, but it would take too long for the various law enforcement agencies to galvanize their efforts and cut off the escape points.

"We're better off driving," Lambert said. "We know which direction he was heading."

His deputy was right. The tire tracks along the shoulder suggested the killer had driven east, but he could be anywhere now. It had taken another five minutes to escape the forest and reach their vehicles.

"It's Adrian Castell."

Lambert turned his head to Thomas. "He's our prime suspect, but all we have to go on are our theories and circumstantial evidence."

"He took Emma, and we know where he's going."

Castell wouldn't go home. Not when there were so many officers trying to find him.

But he might take Emma to where it all started—the abandoned house near the school.

If Thomas followed his hunch, they would have to leave the countryside and return to Wolf Lake. He radioed Aguilar and the state trooper to continue patrolling the roads.

In the meantime, Thomas contacted his deputies and told them where to meet. They would convene at the elementary school and approach the haunted house on foot. By moving through the backyards of neighboring homes, they would take Castell by surprise.

If Castell was the killer.

And if Thomas's theory about the abandoned house held water.

So many potential judgment errors. But he had to be right for Emma, Hannah, and all those poor children Trooper Fitzgerald had uncovered.

"To the elementary school," Thomas said.

Lambert opened his mouth to question Thomas but said nothing. His jaw firmed.

"Let's save Emma."

39

Thomas's hand searched through his pocket. He knew it was here somewhere.

Moving in a crouch behind a row of houses, which stood stark against the moonlit sky, he found the wrapper and undid it with his fingers. He popped the stick of chewing gum in his mouth.

It wasn't a habit he was proud of. But stress was pulling his nerves taut, and he needed a few tricks to release his pent-up energy and stay focused.

Lambert looked back at him. They passed through a yard fronted by a pale-yellow one-story house with motion-activated floodlights. Three more deputies were converging on the abandoned house from the opposite side of the neighborhood, and Kane Grove police had lent a hand, supporting their efforts with two unmarked squad cars parked at either end of the street. Castell wouldn't escape unseen.

Despite his certainty, Thomas hedged his bets. Even now, LeVar and another junior deputy were stationed outside of Castell's residence. So far, no one had come or gone.

"Stop questioning yourself," Lambert said as they scurried ahead.

"What?"

"The chewing gum, the look on your face. You're right about this, Thomas. You always are."

It helped to hear Lambert's support. He remembered what old Sheriff Gray had said.

Five percent knowledge, 95% gut feeling. That's what separates a good cop from someone who sticks his nose in textbooks every day.

Gray had given Thomas a chance and opened the door for an awkward boy with Asperger's. The former sheriff had believed in him.

Just as Thomas believed in Lambert, Aguilar, LeVar, and all his deputies. Had it not been for Lambert's search skills, they wouldn't have found Emma's phone. A few minutes earlier, they might have discovered Emma holding the device.

Castell had struck first, but he couldn't run forever. A net of law enforcement officers enveloped the area, and more were on the way. Everyone was here because they trusted Thomas, though the sheriff couldn't prove Castell was a serial killer or that he'd taken Emma back to Wolf Lake. Back to his old haunt.

In truth, Thomas had every reason to question the theory. If Castell had a shred of sense, he would have driven Emma to another town, another state. But the killer was back, and he was escalating. He no longer thought like a rational human. All that mattered was murder and serving the demons in his head.

The abandoned house came into view.

It was time for Thomas to put his instincts to the test.

~

THE HOUSE STOOD black and silent. Moonlight glimmered against the windows, including two broken panes on the near side of the structure. A porch with warped boards hung off the front. Nothing about the house seemed healthy. Not the punctured roof, the overgrown lawn, or the skeletal tree that butted up against the dingy siding.

There was no mailbox, no family vehicle in the driveway. Only death lurked here.

When Thomas kneeled at the edge of the property, he lifted a pair of binoculars and glassed the house. Lambert did the same. On one hand, the deputy held a radio, which he used to communicate with the three deputies on the far side of the yard. Thomas couldn't see them, but he knew they were there.

Thomas popped another stick of gum in his mouth. On his signal, the team members would converge on the property from either side. He wanted two deputies to enter together through the back door while he and Lambert broke through the front. The third deputy would remain outside, in case Castell made it past them and tried to escape.

Five percent knowledge, 95% gut feeling.

He needed to remind himself. If he was wrong and the killer murdered Emma elsewhere, he would never live this down. The people would vote him out of office. Not that he would run for election after an error this grave.

But he knew in his heart that he was right.

So why didn't he see any movement inside? Law enforcement had checked every vehicle within five blocks of the house, and Castell's car wasn't among them.

He worried at the gum as if it were an itch he couldn't scratch. If only he'd anticipated Emma running from the clearing after the LIDAR discovered so many bodies. He should have been proactive.

But the journalist wasn't supposed to be in the forest. She'd escaped Aguilar and driven there on her own. If only she'd stayed put inside the station where she was safe.

So many events that could have gone differently. Beating himself up wouldn't save Emma or bring those kids back from the dead.

Thomas grabbed his radio. "On my signal."

40

The front door opened without a squeak. That differed from the last time they'd investigated. Had someone oiled the hinges?

Thomas stood beside Lambert. Both officers aimed their guns into the blackness. Lambert focused on the living room while Thomas glanced up the staircase. With two raised fingers, he motioned at his deputy to check out the downstairs. He could hear the other deputies coming through the back entrance.

There was no one to watch his back if he climbed the steps. He was chasing a devil. Alone. This wasn't smart law enforcement.

No sounds came from the second floor. All he heard was his own breathing.

With one hand on the banister, he took the first step. Then the next. Towards evil.

At the top, he sensed someone behind him and swung around. Lambert pressed a finger to his lips.

Now the tall deputy passed Thomas and studied the top floor. Three closed doors. They'd discovered the food bag behind the third.

Still no signs of life. Thomas couldn't afford to be wrong.

Communicating with their eyes, the officers split left and right. Lambert entered an empty bedroom and stalked toward the closet and attached bathroom. Thomas took door number three.

He saw her on the floor. Emma wasn't moving.

Her head lay beside what appeared to be a discarded soda can. Liquid ran between her skull and the drink. He hoped it was soda and not blood.

Seeing Emma ripped him out of the zone. He no longer made rational decisions or thought things through. Nor did he check his blind spots.

The broken board crashed down on the back of his head. His legs wobbled, and he struck the floor with Castell on top of him.

Two hands wrapped around Thomas's neck and squeezed. His legs scrambled, shoes pushing against the floor and seeking purchase.

Adrian Castell grinned down at him. Saliva and a dark substance that might have been blood dripped from his mouth. Thomas's instincts about Castell had been right. And now they would get him killed.

With his eyes drooping shut and his strength waning, Thomas made a fist and struck out in desperation. The punch connected. The killer's head shot backward.

Though the killer maintained the top position, the distraction gave Thomas the chance he needed. The sheriff bucked against Castell's wobbly form and toppled him to the floor.

No sooner did Thomas reach for his gun than Lambert appeared in the doorway. The killer lunged at Thomas, placing the sheriff between himself and Lambert. There was no room for Thomas to lift his service weapon.

With a shout, Thomas hurled the killer against the wall. Castell's head hit the plaster in a puff of smoke.

The impact took the fight out of the child murderer. He twitched on the floor, struggling to regain control of his limbs. Thomas aimed the weapon.

"It's over, Castell."

~

A PAIR of female paramedics huddled beside the prone journalist. Flashlights from the other deputies provided the only illumination.

"She's stable," the first paramedic said.

Thomas closed his eyes and looked skyward. "Thank you."

Castell had knocked Emma unconscious, perhaps to keep her quiet while he warded off the advancing officers.

"You all right, boss man?" Lambert asked.

The deputy's forehead was lined with concern.

"My head hurts something fierce, but I'm not bleeding."

"I want the paramedics to look at you next."

Thomas didn't protest. His deputy wanted to be sure he was okay.

Out the window, he could see Aguilar, who had returned to Wolf Lake, escorting Adrian Castell into a waiting cruiser. Cuffs held the man's wrists behind his back, and two burly Kane Grove PD officers ensured the killer didn't fight back.

"There goes Satan himself," Thomas muttered.

"What's that, boss man?"

"Nothing." He moved away from the window and returned to Emma, careful to give the paramedics space. The journalist wavered in and out of consciousness.

But she was alive. That was all that mattered.

Acting on Lambert's orders, the paramedics escorted Thomas to the ambulance. He would take a ride to the hospital with Emma.

"Do me a favor," Thomas said to Lambert.

"Anything."

"Call Chelsey and tell her I'm all right. If I make the call, she'll think I'm trying to avoid writing wedding invitations."

"Are you sure you're okay, Thomas? You aren't making sense."

Thomas laughed. "Yes, I am. Just let her know I'm okay."

41

Ten minutes after LeVar returned from class, he decided it was too mild for a sweatshirt and jeans. Should he change into shorts? It probably wasn't warm enough, but the temptation pulled him.

Today was the first day of spring. Not according to the calendar, which announced the equinox had passed three days ago. He had his own definition of the changing seasons.

Some considered March 21, the equinox, the beginning of spring. Others drew the line at the first 60-degree day. For LeVar, the season changed when his favorite Wolf Lake ice cream shop opened its doors. He could already taste the triple-scoop strawberry cheesecake stuffed into a waffle cone, the sticky chill as it melted and rolled over his fingers. Soon it would be summer.

He thought better of wearing shorts and settled on blue jeans and a T-shirt. Checking himself in the mirror, he pulled a baseball cap over his head and snaked his dreadlocks through the back opening.

The phone rang. He glanced at the screen. Naomi.

He wondered what she wanted. For a split-second, his back iced over. Had she found out about Scout and LeVar's growing relationship? Naomi wouldn't approve. Not that she should. LeVar felt terrible that things were spinning out of control again.

With caution, he answered.

"LeVar, I'm running late at Shepherd Systems. Can you pick up Scout from school? I hate to impose, but a last-second issue came up, and I need to fix things."

"I can do that. She's not taking the bus today?"

"No. She wants to stop by Wolf Lake Consulting and pick up her paycheck, and there's no one to drive her from our house to the firm."

"Gotcha."

"Plus, she wore a skirt and flats today. I don't want her walking from school to the village center."

He remembered their legs brushing under the desk at Wolf Lake Consulting and how it had made him feel. Like a heel. There was no reason he should interest himself in a teenage girl.

"LeVar, are you there?"

"Sorry, Naomi. I was just thinking. Yeah, I'll pick her up and take her by the office. I'm headed across the village for opening day. Mind if I take Scout?"

"Opening day? This is about ice cream, I take it."

He laughed. "Got me there."

"That's no problem. But don't let her buy an extra-large cone. She'll ruin her appetite for dinner."

He jogged past the A-frame to reach his car. A light was on upstairs, though Chelsey and Thomas were both at work. Emma Walsh was staying here. Thomas didn't want her to leave until she recovered from the abduction.

LeVar thought about knocking and saying hello, but maybe it was better to let Emma deal with the kidnapping and almost dying at the hands of Adrian Castell.

Several blocks from the village center, he pulled in front of the school. This time, he parked far from the buses and waited in the lot. One administrator took pleasure in harassing LeVar. To some people, he would always be a Harmon gangster.

He sent a text to Scout and told her where to meet him. She appeared on the sidewalk. Her dark hair appeared golden in the sunlight, and a breeze kicked up and lifted the skirt to her knees. He averted his eyes and drummed his hands on the wheel. A Tribe Called Quest boomed through the speakers.

"What's up, what's up?" She giggled, sliding into the passenger seat.

"Toss your backpack behind you."

She did.

"Thanks for picking me up."

"Couldn't have you walking to WLC in those shoes. How was school?"

She rolled her eyes. "Long. They made us play kickball in gym class."

"What's wrong with kickball?" he asked.

"Nothing if you enjoy a rubber ball smacking you in the teeth."

"Scout, you're supposed to catch the ball, not bite it."

"You're quite the comedian today."

They stopped at the office so she could pick up her check. The irony struck him—Chelsey and Raven could pay Scout as a private technology contractor, but they couldn't pay him as a PI because New York State said he wasn't old enough to work in private investigations. Oh well. He felt happy for Scout. Someday he might start his own firm.

Not wanting his sister to pull him into working, as she was wont to do, he waited in the car. Scout returned after a brief conversation.

"Got your money?" he asked.

"Hey, a girl's gotta get paid."

"You up for ice cream?"

"Is this opening day? I totally forgot."

"It is, and don't you forget it."

The line extended from the window to the curb when they pulled into the parking lot. No matter. It was worth the wait. A stroke of luck: The owner opened a second window, cutting the time in half. LeVar ordered his large strawberry cheesecake in a waffle cone, and Scout chose maple walnut in a dish with whipped cream on top. She was the one with the big fat paycheck, but he covered the cost. Asking her to pay was wrong.

Away from the crowd, he located a round burgundy picnic bench with an umbrella jutting out of the center. He was the first to sit. She scooted beside him and crossed one leg over the other. In his mind, "Don't Stand So Close to Me" by The Police played in an endless loop.

"How's your maple walnut?" he asked between bites.

She closed her eyes and smiled. "The best. Thanks so much for splurging."

"After the FBI hires you, you'll owe me a cone."

"Deal."

"I realize you were at school today and probably missed last night's news."

Scout looked at him. "Anything exciting?"

"Big time. Not only did we catch Ian Mercer and stop him from making a grave mistake, Thomas and Lambert caught Hannah Clarke's kidnapper."

Her eyes widened into saucers. "Are you serious?"

"Two bad guys in one night."

"Oh my God, LeVar. This is the best news ever!"

She threw her arms around his shoulder. Before he knew what was happening, she planted a kiss on his cheek.

Realizing what she'd done, she slid a few inches away and pushed the hair out of her eyes. "Sorry for getting carried away. It was just a friendship kiss, all right?"

He looked down. "Yeah, I figured that out."

The awkward moment lingered. This conversation was a long time coming.

"You're not mad, are you? I was just so happy that everything worked out."

"Listen, Scout. We need to talk."

From the way the teenager focused on her ice cream and didn't meet his eyes, she seemed to understand she'd done wrong.

"What do you want to talk about?"

"About this," he said, gesturing at how close they sat. "And the kiss. I realize you were reacting because you're happy, but I'm twenty."

"And I'm only sixteen," she said, biting a nail. "I'll always be too young, won't I?"

"Scout, how do you really feel about our relationship? Be honest."

"We're the best of friends."

"Truth," he said. "Forever. You sure there isn't more?"

She looked ready to argue and stopped. "I'd be lying if I said I didn't have feelings for you."

He lost his appetite. "For real?"

"It's wrong, LeVar, but I can't help it. All year, I've dealt with immature boys at school who want my number, and here you are, this amazing, caring, mature dude who lives next door."

"That doesn't make me boyfriend material."

"Yes, it does. Not that it could ever happen, because I'll be sixteen forever."

"Not forever." He touched her arm. "Your friendship means everything to me. I won't risk losing you. Not for the world."

"Same. But tell me you don't have feelings for me too."

He wiped his lips with a napkin. "Scout, I really can't—"

"Remember, LeVar. Honesty."

"Okay, I kinda do. A little. But it's nothing I would ever pursue. If I did, I would disrespect you, your mother, Thomas, and myself."

She gazed into the distance. "What happens in two years when I turn eighteen, or in four when I'm twenty? What if we still feel the same?"

"We'll cross that bridge when the time comes. But, Scout, you'll meet someone between now and then. Probably a lot of guys."

She scoffed. "A lot of immature guys."

"What are we gonna do about this?"

Scout rested an elbow on the table and set her chin on her fist. "For starters, I'll be more careful about how close we sit."

"That's a wise idea."

"Also, I promise not to kiss you, even if it's just a happy smooch on the cheek."

He chuckled. "It's for the best. When we study in your bedroom, the door should stay open. In the guest house, we'll keep the shades up."

"Mom trusts us."

"I intend to keep things that way." He held out a hand. "Best friends?"

She hesitated before accepting his offer. "Yes."

42

Throughout the spring, the Finger Lakes are home to the great blue heron. The gray-blue birds nest along the shore and among the wetlands. The region also hosts osprey and an endless variety of songbirds, their calls a musical background to the sunny days. If you're lucky, you'll spy bald eagles swooping over the water.

It was by the shore that LeVar observed the winged creatures. Some plucked fish out of the water, while more perched on leafless tree limbs that hung over the shore.

He bought an ice cream maker. And a grill insert so he could make wood-fired pizza.

This was the life, and he wouldn't risk his reputation or his friendships by acting upon a secret urge. His mother had taught him better than this.

Still, as he looked at the Mournings' house, glowing in the late afternoon rays, he wondered what would have happened had he not kept Scout at arm's length. Not for the first time, he considered moving. He could rent an apartment near Kane Grove University or live in the dorms. But he would miss Thomas and everyone who supported him.

Ian Mercer was serving time, but he would turn his life around. The technologist had too many skills to allow a crook like Elliot Saunders to take advantage of him.

With Adrian Castell behind bars, the world was safer. The children of Wolf Lake could walk home without fear. And if Thomas got his wish, the village would knock down the abandoned house and start over. A community green space would look nice and give the kids a place to stop after school let out.

No one could explain why Castell had pursued Emma Walsh for so long without trying to abduct her until now. Perhaps something awakened inside the monster and drove him to fulfill his destiny. What was it about Emma that attracted him? LeVar didn't want to know.

He picked up a rock and skipped it across the water. Seven splashes—not bad. Seven didn't beat his record, but he had a lifetime to try again.

Voices pulled his attention to the A-frame. The deck door stood open to the screen. Thomas and Chelsey were hosting Naomi, Scout, Emma, and a few deputies. LeVar heard Aguilar's gruff laughter inside.

They greeted him as soon as he entered. Emma sat at the dining room table with two packed bags by her feet. It seemed she was moving on. Jack, who sensed his new friend was leaving, rested his head on his paws and wore a sad expression. Tigger was nowhere to be seen, but undoubtedly the tabby was near and plotting another caper.

"Glad you made it," Thomas said, clapping LeVar on the shoulder. "Emma is about to leave, and I wanted you to say goodbye."

He hadn't gotten to know Emma as closely as the other deputies who'd worked on her investigation, but they'd spoken enough for him to like the woman. The journalist's spirit inspired him. She didn't know the meaning of failure.

"What will you do now?" LeVar asked.

"Drive home and work on my story," Emma said.

"Is your story about Hannah?"

"And the other girls, yes. I want the world to hear their stories. More than anything, I want everyone to know that, in the end, they won."

"That's a tremendous attitude," Aguilar said.

Chelsey nodded. "After you publish the story, I want to read it."

"It would mean a lot to me if you did," said Emma.

"Keep my number. Anytime you want to reach out and talk, I'm here for you."

"I will. Besides, I want to hear all about the wedding."

Chelsey glanced at a box of invitations on the table and gave Thomas a knowing look. Lambert laughed.

Scout sat beside her mother. The instant her eyes met LeVar's, he looked away. When he turned back to the conversation, he saw Thomas staring. Had the sheriff seen the exchange?

Checking her watch, Emma stood. "Thomas and Chelsey, I can't thank you enough for hosting me. I don't know what I would do without your graciousness."

Everyone exchanged hugs with the journalist, even Lambert and Aguilar. They escorted her to the door and waved goodbye as the car drove away. Upon returning, Chelsey dotted her eyes with a tissue.

Thomas approached. "Hey, why don't we take a walk?"

That was the sheriff's way of saying they needed to talk. LeVar left the others and met Thomas on the porch.

"The trail finally dried out," Thomas said, pointing at the narrow path that led from the shore to the state park. "Want to test it out?"

"Sure, Thomas."

They said little as they climbed the gentle incline. Brown,

spindly brush encroached on the trail, but grass shoots gave the field a splash of green. It seemed more like spring every day.

Thomas stared thoughtfully at LeVar for a moment before speaking.

"You know, back when I was about your age, I had this old pickup truck. It was the first vehicle my parents purchased for me. It wasn't much to look at, but it got me where I needed to go."

"I can't picture you driving a beater."

"Well, I did. One day, the engine started acting up. I figured I could push it a bit longer and avoid the hassle of fixing it. But one evening, coming back from college, it just quit on me. Middle of nowhere, no cell service back then."

Thomas paused, letting the story sink in. He strolled with his hands clasped behind his back. "I ended up walking five miles to the nearest phone. Took me hours. And the whole time, I was thinking, 'Why didn't I just take care of it when I had the chance?' See, I knew there was a problem, but I ignored it, hoping it would sort itself out. Problems never do. It's up to us to make things right."

"Where is this going, Thomas? I'm sure you didn't take me this far to talk about your first truck."

"Point is, sometimes we see a potential problem, and we think, 'Ah, it'll be fine. I can handle it.' But things have a way of coming to a head when we least expect it, especially if we don't address them early."

"Straight up."

Thomas rolled his shoulders and chose his next words carefully. "I noticed the exchange between you and Scout, and it's no secret you spend a lot of time together."

"It was nothing."

"It didn't look like nothing. Scout is a bright young woman, incredibly talented. And you, you've turned your life around in ways most can't even imagine. I admire you. But now isn't the time. Maybe it will be several years down the road. I just want to ensure you're thinking things through. Not just for now, but how today's decisions will affect your future. Are you following me, LeVar?"

Warmth built in LeVar's chest. He'd never formed a relationship with his birth father. Thomas was the man he wanted to become.

"I hear you."

"You've grown a lot since you first walked into my life. That's not something many can do under your circumstances."

LeVar shifted uncomfortably, remembering his mother almost dying from a heroin overdose before Thomas saved her. "I've had good people to look up to."

"As Father often said, 'Don't blow a long-term investment for short-term gains.'"

"Scout and I, we're just friends. She's got her path, and I've got mine. We're both aware of where we should draw the line."

"That's encouraging to hear," said Thomas. "I trust you. But remember, life's paths can sometimes veer unexpectedly. It's how you navigate the hairpin turn that defines you. Make sure you both look out for those markers, *aight*?"

"You're stealing my line again, Thomas. For the record, you don't have to worry about me crossing any lines. Scout is a sister to me. I have too much respect for her and Naomi to jeopardize that."

"I know you do. Just remember, being a good man means making tough choices for the right reasons. Don't let problems sneak up on you, and you'll never find yourself stranded in the middle of nowhere."

LeVar shook his head. "Is it true that they didn't have cell phones back then?"

"I'm not *that* old, LeVar."

A fish leaped and sent concentric circles across the lake. In the soft glow of the setting sun, they turned around and descended the trail, leaving the air filled with unspoken understanding and mutual respect.

LeVar pondered the future. A year from now, he'd wrap up his junior year at Kane Grove University. Scout would join him soon after, and their decisions would require greater care and precision. He decided that no matter what, he would move forward with integrity and love.

In Wolf Lake, as in life, the journey was everything. And it was just beginning.

GET A FREE BOOK!

I'm a pretty nice guy once you look past the grisly images in my head. Most of all, I love connecting with awesome readers like you.

Join my VIP Reader Group and get a FREE serial killer thriller for your Kindle.

Get My Free Book

www.danpadavona.com/thriller-readers-vip-group/

SUPPORT YOUR FAVORITE AUTHORS

Did you enjoy this book? If so, please let other thriller fans know by leaving a short review. Positive reviews help spread the word about independent authors and their novels. Thank you.

Copyright Information

Published by Dan Padavona

Visit my website at www.danpadavona.com

Cover Design by Caroline Teagle Johnson

Created with Vellum

ACKNOWLEDGMENTS

No writer journeys alone. Special thanks are in order to my editor, C.B. Moore, for providing invaluable feedback, catching errors, and making my story shine. I also wish to thank my brilliant cover designer, Caroline Teagle Johnson. Your artwork never ceases to amaze me. I owe so much of my success to your hard work. Shout outs to my advance readers, including Kylie Martin, Ted Browne, and Marcia Campbell, for catching those final pesky typos and plot holes. Most of all, thank you to my readers for your loyalty and support. You changed my life, and I am forever grateful.

ABOUT THE AUTHOR

Dan Padavona is the author of The Nia Carter series, The Wolf Lake series, The Thomas Shepherd series, The Logan and Scarlett series, The Darkwater Cove series, The Scarlett Bell thriller series, *Her Shallow Grave*, and The Dark Vanishings series. He lives in upstate New York with his beautiful wife, Terri, and their children, Joe, and Julia. Dan is a meteorologist with NOAA's National Weather Service. Besides writing, he enjoys visiting amusement parks, beach vacations, Renaissance fairs, gardening, playing with the family dogs, and eating too much ice cream.

Visit Dan at: www.danpadavona.com

Printed in Great Britain
by Amazon

44427021R00148